PUFFIN BOOKS

Frank and the New Narkiz

Livi Michael has two sons, Paul and Ben, a dog called Jenny and a hamster called Frank. She has written books for adults before, but ever since getting to know Frank has had the sense that he had a story that should be told. So here it is, and both Livi and Frank hope you enjoy it very much.

LIVI MICHAEL

Frank
and
the
New
Narkiz

Illustrated by Derek Brazell

PUFFIN

Books by Livi Michael

FRANK AND THE BLACK HAMSTER OF NARKIZ
FRANK AND THE CHAMBER OF FEAR
FRANK AND THE FLAMES OF TRUTH
FRANK AND THE NEW NARKIZ

THE WHISPERING ROAD

To Freya and Joe, and to friends of Frank everywhere!

And a special thanks to Judith Murray, for information and advice about the Countryside Agency

PUFFIN BOOKS

Published by the Penguin Group
Penguin Books Ltd, 80 Strand, London WC2R 0RL, England
Penguin Group (USA) Inc., 375 Hudson Street, New York, New York 10014, USA
Penguin Group (Canada), 10 Alcorn Avenue, Toronto, Ontario, Canada M4V 3B2
(a division of Pearson Penguin Canada Inc.)
Penguin Ireland, 25 St Stephen's Green, Dublin 2, Ireland (a division of Penguin Books Ltd)
Penguin Group (Australia), 250 Camberwell Road, Camberwell, Victoria 3124, Australia
(a division of Pearson Australia Group Pty Ltd)
Penguin Books India Pvt Ltd, 11 Community Centre, Panchsheel Park, New Delhi – 110 017, India
Penguin Group (NZ), cnr Airborne and Rosedale Roads, Albany, Auckland 1310, New Zealand
(a division of Pearson New Zealand Ltd)
Penguin Books (South Africa) (Pty) Ltd, 24 Sturdee Avenue, Rosebank,
Johannesburg 2196, South Africa

Penguin Books Ltd, Registered Offices: 80 Strand, London WC2R 0RL, England

www.penguin.com

First published 2005
1

Text copyright © Livi Michael, 2005
Illustrations copyright © Derek Brazell, 2005
All rights reserved

The moral right of the author and illustrator has been asserted

Set in 13/15pt Monotype Bembo
Made and printed in England by Clays Ltd, St Ives plc

British Library Cataloguing in Publication Data
A CIP catalogue record for this book is available from the British Library

ISBN 0–141–31700–0

Contents

Foreword

This is a story about a hamster called Frank, who lives at number 13 Bright Street, with his Owner, Guy. Most hamsters do live with their Owners, but at one time, not very long ago, they lived wild and free beneath the Syrian sands, in a territory they called Narkiz. Frank is a hamster who feels the Call of The Wild. He likes to get out of his cage and explore.

The very first time Frank got out, he heard the Call of the mysterious being known as the Black Hamster of Narkiz. Since then, he has met him several times, and the Black Hamster has told Frank that he needs him to help his people, and Frank hopes that one day he will lead all hamsters to Freedom.

There are other hamsters on Bright Street. Mabel is a proud, snowy white hamster who lives next door to Frank. Elsie lives at number 3 Bright Street. She is Mabel's cub, though Mabel never took very good care of her. She is a practical, tidy hamster who is very fond of her Owner, Lucy, and of her twin brother, George.

George used to live next door to Elsie, at number 5 Bright Street, but on one adventure George met a hamster called Daisy, and they decided to live together in The Wild, a stretch of waste ground facing the houses of Bright Street. There they made a refuge for hamsters, shrews, moles, field mice and any other creature who needed it, and when Frank saw the new territory, he realized that it resembled the ancient homeland of Narkiz.

George's place on Bright Street has been taken by a hamster called Maurice, from the pet shop. He is a rather disagreeable hamster who doesn't like adventures, and so Maurice and Frank don't get on very well.

The other thing you need to know is that Frank has a motto. His motto is 'Courage', and when he says it to himself it always seems to have an exclamation mark after it, like this, 'Courage!'

1 Frank's Dream

It was nearly Christmas. Frank had never experienced Christmas before, and was rather confused by it. Guy arrived home dragging a small tree, which he put up right in front of Frank's cage. The tip of one of the branches poked through the bars of his cage and made him sneeze.

'Why ever does he want a tree in his living room?' Frank wondered.

Next, Guy decorated the tree with glass baubles and coloured lights, and there was much muttering of bad language under his breath as the lights flickered once, then failed to work. Guy changed the plug and screwed some of the lights back in properly, and eventually they lit the whole room with a soft, spangled glow. He put up a wreath and a candle, then exhausted by his efforts, fell asleep.

'Oi!' Frank thought. 'What about my food?'

But Guy was already snoring peacefully.

The weather got colder and the hours of daylight shrank. Each morning, the postman arrived with cards that Guy put up all over the room, and which toppled over again almost immediately. Guy rehearsed carols on his guitar, so that he could get everyone to join in singing at the pub. The carols were about babies and angels and snow, which was something that Frank had never seen.

'They're all about your part of the world,' he said to Frank. 'Jordan, Syria, Israel.'

A great pang went through Frank when he heard those names. Of course, Frank had never been to any of those countries himself. They were hot countries, though, he felt sure. He couldn't imagine that they ever had any snow. He felt quite excited at the thought that they might have snow here, and each morning he sniffed anxiously at the window, but there was only rain.

Guy went out a lot on the days leading up to Christmas, to the pub, or to his mum's house, or to one of his new, guitar-playing friends. Frank was left on his own with the sparkling tree that made the room look so different, full of shadows. It would be the perfect time to get out and explore, but strangely, Frank didn't want to. He felt sleepy and spent more and more time curled up in his bed. Then one morning Guy woke him up unusually early.

'Merry Christmas, Frank,' he said, and there, wrapped up in his cage with blue ribbon, was a miniature corn on the cob of his very own.

Frank didn't have anything for Guy, of course, but Guy seemed happy enough unwrapping some new frets for his bass guitar, some CDs and a new songbook. He sat down and composed a song to Frank right away:

It's Christmas Day
And you're with me
That's better than the presents
Round the Christmas tree . . .

And Guy went on singing while the room filled
with the smell of bacon and eggs and he made toast
and marmalade for Frank. Then after breakfast, Guy
brought out one more present, a large box with
pictures of space rockets on the wrapping paper.

'This is for Jake and Josh,' he said. 'It's a construction
set. But I don't know if I want to take it round now.'

Guy looked nervous and worried. Frank liked Jackie, but the last thing he wanted to do was to encourage Guy's feelings, because that would mean the boys would start coming round and playing with Frank as enthusiastically as they had once played with George. Their idea of Fun with George had been a key factor in George's decision to live in The Wild, and Frank couldn't say that he blamed him. But now here was Guy, looking suddenly rather depressed and unsure of himself. And it was Christmas.

'Go on,' he said to Guy. 'You can't not give it to them, now you've bought it.'

'I don't know,' said Guy. 'Suppose Matchless Mick's there?'

'Suppose he isn't?' said Frank. 'You won't know unless you go round.'

Guy looked scared. 'I could always give the construction kit to Luke,' he said (Luke was his nephew).

'Look,' said Frank. 'What's the worst that could happen?'

Guy and Frank often had conversations like this. Ever since the end of Frank's first adventure, he had found that if Guy wasn't concentrating or thinking too hard, which was most of the time, Frank could speak into his thoughts and get him to do things. Initially Frank had rather abused this power, by making Guy stand in the corner of the room with a lampshade on his head, or pull hideous faces at people through the window, but he had soon learned that the power was too important to be wasted, and these days, he hardly used it at all. But now, well, Guy *had* just got him a Christmas present.

'Go to see her,' he said directly into Guy's thoughts.

Guy stared at the wall for several moments, but then muttering to himself 'Why not?' and 'What harm can it do?', he picked up the present and left the house. Moments later, he was back looking really pleased.

'She's invited me over for a drink later on,' he said. 'Along with a few of the neighbours,' he added hastily, in case Frank should think it was a date.

So that was Christmas. Guy was out a lot, the weather was dull and rainy, Frank slept. Then there were more celebrations at New Year. There was singing at the pub that even Frank could hear well into the night, and at midnight there were fireworks, though happily not many of them. Frank couldn't see what all the fuss was about. What the humans called 'New Year' just seemed part of the general seasonal change that Frank could sense even though he was indoors.

It was as though the earth was drawing into itself, like a snail going into its shell. It was the time when plants put down roots and stored food, and animals flew south or hibernated. That was the main thing Frank felt now, the urge to sleep. He slept all day and well into the night. And while he slept he had many dreams: about Narkiz and about his past adventures; about Humphrey and the Knights of Urr; about Chestnut in the sewers and about mad Vince. He dreamed about the first time he had ever escaped into The Wild, where he had seen in a vision the full power and glory of his tribe, and he dreamed about his mother, Leila, whom he could hardly remember. And continually throughout his dreams, there was the presence of the Black Hamster, sometimes just out of sight, sometimes far ahead, with Frank following. He dreamed of the coming of great machines, and the destruction of the Old Narkiz, or was it the New Narkiz? The surroundings looked surprisingly familiar and he could see the line of houses that was Bright Street. But before he had time to investigate, his dream changed and there was Leila, unhappy and alone, in human hands, and crying out to him, 'Frank!'

Alone in his bed Frank sweated and struggled to wake, and again a voice spoke in his ear, 'Frank, wake up.'

Frank managed to prise open an eye, and what he saw was the thickest, velvety black pelt. He closed his eye again, then forced them both open.

There, in his cage, was the Black Hamster of Narkiz.

Full of relief that he wasn't still dreaming, and joy at seeing him again, Frank clambered out of his bed and went to greet his old friend. But the first words the Black Hamster spoke caused all Frank's relief and joy to drain away.

'Frank,' he said. 'There is Danger.'

2 Mabel's Dream

Mabel had a wonderful Christmas. First there had been all the presents: a new buggy shaped like a chariot, a little mirror for her cage so that she could admire herself; some special scented powder to give her pelt that extra sheen, and lots of new toys and playthings — and *then* there had been all the food. Turkey and cranberry sauce, stuffing and roast potatoes, apple pie. At last, she thought, her humans, who had been a bit preoccupied lately, had started to treat her the way she deserved. The feasting continued until Boxing Day, and then only a few days elapsed before it started all over again. Mabel got an extra set of presents at New Year, since this was her official birthday, and she even had a tiny cake, baked by Tania. Outside the days were short, cold and dark, and soon Mabel, brimming with food and entirely contented, felt a growing urge to sleep.

She was wakened by the sound of strange voices in her living room.

'Is this your hamster? My word, she *is* rather special, isn't she?'

Whoever it was obviously had taste. Mabel uncurled herself in a leisurely way, then climbed out of her bed for a closer look. A pair of green eyes, almost like a cat's, glowed down at her.

'My goodness, she's a splendid size, isn't she?' said the voice.

'Is she white all over?' said a man's voice.

'*Dazzling*,' said the woman.

'Have you really never thought of showing her?' said the man.

Mabel simpered and preened, all the time keeping one eye on her admirers. Even from her limited perspective the woman who was gazing so appreciatively at her was rather a striking sight herself: blonde curls piled into an amazing bouffant, and the longest claws she had ever seen on a human, painted a glittering green like her eyes. She was obviously a very important person. Not like Mrs Wheeler, Tania's mum. Mrs Wheeler had aspirations and did her best, Mabel supposed, but lately she had been looking, well, rather unravelled. A stray thread here, a wisp of hair there, the frayed edges of collars and cuffs, whereas this woman looked as if she had never in her life had a single hair out of place.

'Look at those incisors!' said the man. 'I could do some work on those.'

The man was altogether a poorer specimen than the woman: shorter and balding, with a neck that reminded Mabel of the neck of a turkey – long, with a lot of loose skin and a prominent bump in the middle of it that bobbed up and down as he spoke.

'There's no doubt about it,' said the woman. 'If you entered her into any of these shows, she'd walk away with the prizes, wouldn't she, Vernon?'

The man nodded vigorously and his bump bobbed up and down, as though a chunk of food had stuck there.

'Absolutely,' he said.

'And that's a lot of money,' the woman said.

Tania's mother touched the stray threads of her hair. 'Really?' she said nervously. 'H-How much?'

'Oh, a lot,' the woman said. 'It varies from show to show. But you could enter her into any number of them in the course of a year. We'd take her for you, up and down the country. And it needn't stop there. There's the international scene as well. You should see the shows at Versailles.'

'Or Milan,' the man put in.

'And Prague,' added the woman. 'Oh, there's a whole career for her out there. And you needn't do a thing. Just sit back and allow us to manage it for you.'

She flashed a gold-edged card towards Mrs Wheeler.

MARCIA TAYLOR

RODENT BEAUTICIAN

---

it stated in fine gold lettering.

'And this is my colleague's card,' she said, holding

out a silver-edged card that was in all other respects similar to her own.

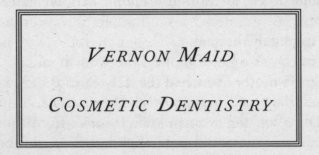

VERNON MAID

COSMETIC DENTISTRY

this card said.

'And this is how you contact us,' the woman said, handing over a black card with gold lettering, which read:

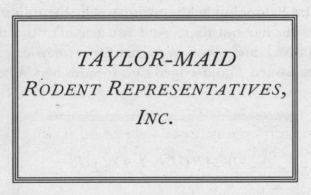

TAYLOR-MAID
RODENT REPRESENTATIVES,
INC.

and listed their contact details.

'Though in fact we'll be in the area tomorrow,' Marcia said, standing up, 'so we'll call in then and see if you've had a chance to think it over. Remember, you don't have to do a thing.'

'Just lie back and count the euros,' said Vernon, and

they both laughed, looking, for a moment, surprisingly alike.

Then they were gone, leaving Mrs Wheeler in a dream. She wandered around the front room touching her hair and muttering, 'Count the euros,' to herself from time to time.

Mrs Wheeler had never liked living in Bright Street. When they had first moved there she had told herself that it was only temporary, until Mr Wheeler's promotion came through. But that had been before Tania was born, and Mr Wheeler's promotion never had come through. Now her first thought was that with the extra money they could move to a better part of town, or even to a cottage by the sea. Mrs Wheeler had always wanted a cottage by the sea. She sat in front of Mabel, looking at the pristine pelt that might earn them so much money.

'But I don't know what Tania will say,' she murmured.

'Bother Tania,' said Mabel. 'I'm going to be on show – all over the world.'

And for a moment she could have sworn that Mrs Wheeler had understood.

'Just think of it!' she said, glowing quite pink. 'Paris, Milan and Prague!'

'Exactly,' Mabel said. 'Just pack me some decent nosh and you can phone them up now. Tell them you've thought it over already. You can deal with Tania when she gets in.'

But Mrs Wheeler hesitated. 'I don't know,' she said. 'Maybe I had better discuss it with Tania first.'

'Typical,' snorted Mabel. 'You could have me out of the house before she even got home. Just get on with it! You humans are such gutless wonders!'

But to tell the truth, Mrs Wheeler was a little bit nervous of Tania and the passions she flew into when she didn't get her own way. She wasn't so nervous of her husband, but he did tend to take Tania's side. Something told her that neither of them would be too happy if she just sent Mabel off.

'I'd better just wait till they're back,' she said, and Mabel rolled her eyes theatrically, but Mrs Wheeler wouldn't be moved. 'You don't know what they'll say,' she said, and she retreated into the kitchen away from Mabel's stony glare.

'No way,' said Tania promptly. 'She's *my* hamster.'

'You don't know anything about these people, love,' said Mr Wheeler when he came in. 'How do you know they'll bring her back?'

'She's not going,' said Tania, 'And that's that.'

In vain Mrs Wheeler protested about the money, and how nice and, well, *professional* the two callers had seemed. And they had been so impressed with Mabel.

'I don't care!' shouted Tania. 'SHE'S NOT GOING!'

Mrs Wheeler could sense one of Tania's tantrums coming on and retired to bed early with a headache. Tania went round to Lucy's, slamming the door on the way, and Mr Wheeler read the paper in the kitchen, leaving Mabel alone in the front room – furious.

'So they think they can stand in my way, do they?'

she said to herself, baring her impressive teeth. 'We'll soon see about that!'

Already Mabel could see her name in lights: images of a white hamster flashing along the boulevards of Paris. She had seen glamorous models on the catwalk (what a name for it!) on Tania's TV, and when she fell asleep she dreamed that she was parading up and down a lush red carpet, to thunderous applause.

The next day, Marcia Taylor and Vernon Maid called round again. They stood at the door smiling toothily at Mrs Wheeler, until she explained to them regretfully that Mabel was her daughter's hamster and Tania didn't want to let her go.

'I see,' said Mrs Taylor thoughtfully, then she whipped out her chequebook and a long golden pen from her handbag. 'Does she want money in advance?'

Mrs Wheeler eyed the chequebook longingly, then swallowed.

'I'm afraid not,' she said. 'She really isn't interested at all.'

Behind them Mabel rattled the bars at the top of her cage. Vernon glanced at her. 'Such a fine specimen,' he said. 'Do you mind if I have another look?'

'Well,' said Mrs Wheeler, but Vernon was already crossing the living room to Mabel's cage. 'Hello, my fine one, my beauty,' he said. 'Do you want to come out for a minute?'

Marcia Taylor beamed at Mrs Wheeler. 'He has such a way with them,' she said, and she too walked past Mrs Wheeler towards Mabel's cage.

This was Mabel's big chance. With both of them

looking at her she was determined to show off her special skills. She stood on her little platform and pirouetted slowly.

'Did you see that?' said Vernon to Marcia.

'Amazing,' said Marcia.

Then Mabel drew herself up to her full height and,

extending her paws, turned the left one up and the right one down. She began to jiggle slowly and rhythmically, shifting from one foot to the other and rotating her hips. Mrs Wheeler watched open-mouthed as she performed the special dance she had done for Frank the first time they had met.

'*Well!*' said Marcia, but Mabel hadn't finished yet. Folding her forepaws on her chest, she pointed the toes of first one paw then the other, stepping round the little platform in a circular motion, without ever taking her eyes off her audience. Marcia, Vernon and Mrs Wheeler gazed at her, entranced. It was rather hypnotic. And when she had finished, she sank down in a deep curtsy.

Vernon expelled a long, slow breath. 'Would you look at that?' he said.

Marcia flicked the pages of her chequebook rapidly. 'That hamster,' she said, 'is a living goldmine. You can't tell me now that you still want to keep her here.'

Mrs Wheeler sat down with her mouth still open. She closed it, then opened it again. 'I've never seen her do that before,' she said weakly. 'Never!'

'That hamster's a natural,' said Vernon. 'I've never come across anything like it.'

'So you'll let us take her,' said Marcia, as if it was quite decided.

Mrs Wheeler looked at them both, bewildered. 'But – Tania,' she said.

Vernon Taylor sat by her side and took her hand.

'Mrs Wheeler,' he said. 'What we have just seen may never have been seen before. It could change the way people think about rodents. Once in a lifetime, Mrs Wheeler,' he went on solemnly, raising a hand as Mrs Wheeler started to speak, 'once in many lifetimes, something so special, so outstanding, happens that it changes the course of history. Landing on the moon, discovering the wheel. When that happens, Mrs Wheeler, that glorious event, do you think it's for the eyes of a few people only? Did the scientists say "Oh, yes, Neil Armstrong did land on the moon, but we forgot to mention it"? No! Those events – those unprecedented, unrepeatable events – belong to the whole world, not just to you and me. This hamster, Mrs Wheeler – your hamster Mavis –'

'Mabel,' said Mrs Wheeler faintly.

'Mabel, your hamster,' said Vernon and paused impressively, 'belongs to the world.'

'Well, but –' said Mrs Wheeler obstinately.

'So, this is what we'll do,' said Mrs Taylor, who had been scribbling calculations rapidly. 'We'll take her, just for the night. You're in luck, because there's a show tomorrow, and we can bring her back tomorrow evening – Tania won't even notice she's gone. We'll try her out at the show, just to demonstrate to you that she'll take all the prizes. And if she doesn't, then we'll go away and never bother you again. But if she does, then you'll be able to prove to your daughter that her hamster could make your fortune.'

Mrs Taylor finished scribbling in her chequebook, ripped a cheque out and handed it to Mrs Wheeler. Mrs Wheeler had been about to protest that of course Tania would notice, she played with Mabel every evening, but when she saw the amount on the cheque, her mouth fell open for the second time. And then she remembered that Tania was having a sleepover that night, and so probably *wouldn't* notice. And Vernon was already dismantling the cage . . .

'No, really, look,' she said, and she got up as if to stop him. 'I'm really not sure. I need time to think. I – I'm not sure it's in Mabel's best interests . . .'

Mrs Taylor sighed in exasperation, but Vernon said, 'I'll tell you what. Why don't we let Mabel decide.' And he lifted the lid off Mabel's cage.

Immediately Mabel climbed out and walked straight on to Vernon's palm. She stood upright, staring beadily around as if saying, 'Well, what are we waiting for?' The look on her face said that if she'd had any bags, she would have packed them. Mrs Wheeler blinked.

'It looks like Mabel knows what she wants,' smiled Marcia Taylor. 'I told you Vernon had a way with rodents. Now if you'll just sign here –'

'Well . . .' said Mrs Wheeler. 'I suppose Tania is staying with a friend after school . . .'

'She won't notice a thing,' said Vernon, petting Mabel, who seemed most uncharacteristically happy to be petted. Usually she bit.

'Well,' said Mrs Wheeler again, but Marcia was already putting the pen in her hand. Somewhat in a daze she signed the paper, and Mrs Taylor packed it away with a flourish. 'Don't you worry about a thing,' she said. 'Come on, Vernon.'

Vernon dropped Mabel into his specially designed travel cage, and both of them hurried to the door. Mrs

Wheeler hurried after them, feeling already that she might have done something very wrong, and that another one of her headaches was coming on.

'You will bring her back, won't you?' she called after them as they revved the engine of an immaculate sports car. 'I'll be waiting tomorrow – don't forget!'

But they had already gone.

3 Danger

Frank stared at the space where the Black Hamster had been. He simply wasn't there any more. He ran around his cage sniffing, at first puzzled, then cross. Was he playing some kind of game?

'Where are you?' he demanded. 'What's going on?'

What a way to be woken up, he thought. He hadn't seen the Black Hamster for ages. He was used to him coming and going, but to simply appear and disappear again – that was odd. And what did he mean, Danger?

'I need a bit more information,' he said aloud.

Nothing.

Frank wondered if he'd been dreaming. At the back of his mind, though, there niggled the memory of what the Black Hamster had said to him towards the end of his last adventure. He had said that the old ways had gone now, and the new ways were beginning. He, the Black Hamster, belonged to the old ways, to the time when hamsters had lived wild, courageous and free. Now they had all had to adjust, one way or another, to living with humans. Frank hadn't wanted to dwell on this because it was as if the Black Hamster had been telling him that his time was over. Then, when Frank had addressed the new colony of hamsters in The Wild, it was as though he had felt the Black Hamster speaking from inside him, which had never happened before. Could it be that Frank would have to learn to communicate with him in a different way?

Frank didn't want to communicate with the Black Hamster in a different way. He wanted to see *more* of him, not less.

'Please come back,' he said. The curtains stirred and Frank looked wildly towards them, but there was nothing, and no one.

Disappointed, Frank turned back to his bed, but not without a final glance over his shoulder. 'I must have been dreaming,' he thought sadly, and he rubbed his paws over his face a few times and groomed his whiskers, just to give the Black Hamster one last chance; then he climbed back into his bedding and curled up tight.

But just as he was falling asleep, the voice came, clear and unmistakable, from somewhere deep inside Frank.

'Go to the pet shop,' it said.

At once Frank was alert, poking a twitching nose out of his bedding.

'What? What?' he said. 'Where are you? Come out and speak to me.'

He ran round his cage once more, peering into all the corners of the room, then he stood quite still and listened. Faintly and further away, but still inside him somewhere, he heard the voice again, like an echo: 'Go to the pet shop.'

'OK,' Frank said. 'Right. Hmm . . .' and he paused for

a moment, distracted. For the pet shop was a long way away, and Frank hadn't been there for a long time – not since Guy had bought him, in fact, when he was a cub. He had led some other hamsters towards it once, through the sewers, but he hadn't actually been back there himself. And that had been in summer, and now it was winter, and all the pipes would be freezing. Besides, it was morning now; Frank could see grey light through the curtains and hear Guy stirring upstairs. Morning was the time when hamsters went to sleep. Frank definitely felt sleepy. He had been tired all week, and one eye was a bit gummed up. He was sure he could feel a cold coming on. For the first time in his life he didn't actually feel *up* to an adventure.

'You couldn't tell me why, could you,' he said hopefully, 'or how?' When there was no reply he said, 'Well, look. I'm going to catch up on my sleep a bit now, but I'll bear in mind what you've said, and when I'm awake, maybe you can tell me some more, or – or give me a sign or something. OK?'

In the silence Frank thought he could hear the faintest sigh. It's all very well, he thought, as he climbed back into bed, sending me on a huge journey in the middle of winter, with no idea why. He curled up tightly. I don't know why he can't come and see me properly. Appearing out of nowhere like that, saying '*Danger!*' It's enough to give a chap a heart attack. Frank closed his eyes tightly.

'Courage!' said the voice.

'Now, that's enough!' said Frank, jumping out of bed so quickly he banged his head on the roof of his cage.

'Come out and show yourself at once! Stop messing about!'

When there was no response to this, Frank thought hard.

'Look,' he said. 'You want me to go to the pet shop. But I can't get through the pipes at this time of year, and I don't know my way by road, and there's all the traffic. I'm not saying I won't go, OK? But would you mind just giving me a clue as to how?'

And at that very moment there was a sharp rap on the door.

Frank almost leapt out of his skin. Guy shouted, 'Coming!' and hurried down the stairs. He opened the door and there was a blast of freezing air. It was much colder now than it had been over Christmas and New Year. Jackie stood on the doorstep, shivering. Frank shivered too and tucked himself back into a pile of woodshavings.

'I just came to say thank you for the construction set,' said Jackie. 'The kids love it, they really do.'

'Come in,' said Guy, opening the door even wider, so that all Frank's woodshavings blew about, and he curled himself up even more tightly.

'Oh, no thanks,' Jackie said. 'I'm just on my way to the pet shop.'

Frank sat bolt upright.

'I've just realized that we've run out of hamster food,' Jackie went on. 'Poor old Maurice doesn't get up much these days, and it's easy to forget he's there.'

It was as if Frank's heart was playing a drum roll. This was it, his sign *and* his clue. He couldn't ignore it any longer. Somehow he had to go to the pet shop with Jackie. Already he was prising the lid off his cage. If only he could get to her before she disappeared!

'Say something, Guy!' he thought urgently.

'You know, I think I might be out of hamster food too,' Guy said. 'I'll just go and check.'

'Perfect!' Frank thought, running along the ledge beneath the gas fire. 'I'll have to get inside her bag or something –'

'Do you want me to get you some?' Jackie said as Guy returned, beaming, and Frank dropped down from the ledge.

'Oh, er, well – I thought – I mean,' Guy said as Frank trotted across the carpet as fast as he could. 'I fancy a bit of fresh air myself – if you don't mind me coming with you.'

Jackie hugged her coat more tightly around her as Frank stopped crossing the carpet and began climbing the settee instead. Guy's jacket was draped over the back of the settee.

'Well, hurry up then,' Jackie was saying. 'It's freezing out here.'

Just as Frank made it all the way to the top of the settee, Guy picked up his jacket and swung it over his shoulder.

'No!' Frank squeaked, but Guy was too intent on Jackie to take any notice.

It was time for Frank's best tactic, the Lightning Twist Propulsion Manoeuvre, that enabled him to jump a long way in emergencies. He took a deep breath, contracted all his muscles, and leapt.

'Now where did I put my key,' said Guy, swinging round so that Frank missed and plummeted to the floor. 'It's here somewhere, I know it is.'

Frank lay where he was, stunned. 'Get up!' he told himself. 'Get up!'

'Here it is!' said Guy, striding towards the door. Frank struggled to his feet. He just managed to clutch the lace from one of Guy's trainers and clamber on to his foot as Guy stepped outside.

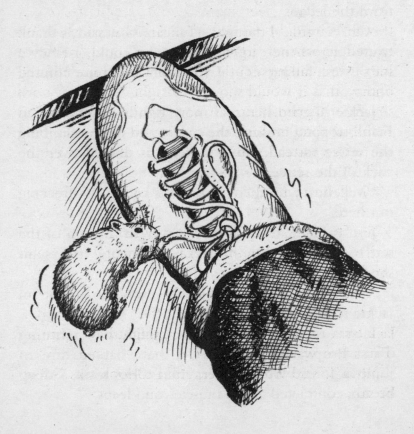

'Don't you want a scarf or something?' Jackie asked. 'It's really cold.'

'I'll be fine,' Guy said, and Frank gasped as he swung his leg off the step. Then, as Guy set off with Jackie, Frank began the difficult task of climbing up Guy's jeans towards his pocket. Fortunately they were old jeans, fashionably ripped and frayed, and Frank clung to the threads with all his paws and his teeth, very much afraid that he would fall off into the road.

He had never been outside in such bitter cold. Over Christmas, the weather had been mild and damp, but now there was sleet in the wind and it looked as though it might snow. Frank had seen snow on television, when it looked to him as though a lot of stars were falling gently to earth. He remembered hoping that it would snow on Bright Street, but now, struggling grimly up Guy's jeans, with the wind whistling through him and making his paws freeze and his teeth chatter so that he could hardly hold on, he changed his mind. He jolted and bumped against Guy's leg, but fortunately Guy was too taken up with Jackie to notice.

'How's Mick?' he asked her. Mick was Jackie's boyfriend, but she didn't seem to want to talk about him.

'Oh, well, you know,' she said.

'Haven't you seen him recently?' Guy ventured. Jackie shook her head. 'I think he might have gone his own sweet way,' she said.

'*Really?*' said Guy, then he tried to look sad. 'Sorry,' he said.

'Oh, well, I think we just wanted different things,' Jackie said. 'He didn't want to settle down; I didn't want to live on the road. Not with the children, anyway.' She sighed.

By this time Frank had reached Guy's knee, but his paws felt as though they might be freezing off, and the sound of traffic was increasing so that he could hardly think. He felt as though he was climbing the north face of a really temperamental mountain that kept trying to fling him off. He was jolted forward every time Guy's leg swung back, and flapped vigorously about in the wind as it came forward again (Guy wore baggy jeans).

'Make them stop somewhere, please!' he begged, without knowing quite who he was asking. But just at that moment they did stop, on the kerb of the main road, just long enough for Frank to scramble up the rest of the way to Guy's pocket, flatten himself and sink thankfully inside. He slid a long way down before realizing that the bottom of the pocket had come unstitched, so that he was actually sliding back down Guy's leg. No wonder he keeps losing things, Frank thought. Sinking his teeth into the fabric he crawled upwards again with determination. At least it was warmer there, and there were some interesting things stuck to the inside of the pocket – a great wodge of chewing gum covered in tissue, a hunk of hair caught up on an inside button and a boiled sweet stuck to the lining. There was some crumpled shiny paper, several old bus tickets and some nuts and bolts that fell clanking to the floor as Frank scrambled past. At last he found the rim of the pocket and, clinging to it, poked his nose out just in time to see that they were approaching Mr Wiggs's pet shop.

'There now, that wasn't too difficult, was it?' said the voice inside.

Frank was speechless.

Jackie caught hold of Guy's arm. 'It's those two funny people again,' she said, as a vivid green sports car flashed past.

'What funny people?' said Guy, looking around as though he expected to see two clowns.

'A man and a woman; they came round asking if I was interested in putting Maurice in for some shows, but I didn't like the look of them. I just said no, thank you, and I was on my way to work. But they were really persistent. They said it paid good money.'

Both Frank and Guy pricked up their ears.

'Cash?' said Guy, trying not to sound too interested.

'I wouldn't know. I sent them away. You can't be too careful these days. Look what happened with that mad bloke, Vince. Didn't they call at your house?'

'They might have done,' said Guy vaguely. 'I was probably busy.'

'Asleep, you mean,' said Jackie, opening the door of the pet shop.

At once Frank was overwhelmed by an array of different scents and memories. He had been born in the pet shop and had lived for the first few weeks of his life amongst a warm squirming litter of hamster cubs. He hardly thought about them now, though sometimes he did suffer pangs of loss. And on one of his adventures he had shared a memory with an elderly hamster called Chestnut, of his mother, Leila, whom he missed very much. Now, as all the different scents of pet food and rabbits and parrots and guinea pigs met him, he felt a wave of nostalgia. He peered round and saw the tank where the hamsters were usually kept. Somehow, he had to make sure that he got himself into that tank.

Mr Wiggs hurried out from the back of the shop.

'Hello, hello!' he said. He knew Jackie and Guy quite well. 'What can I do for you?'

'A bag of hamster food, please,' said Jackie, and Guy went over to peer at the guinea pigs.

'Ahh, aren't they lovely,' he said. 'I always wanted a guinea pig when I was a boy.'

The guinea pigs were kept in a cage with bars rather than a glass tank, so this was Frank's chance. As soon as Guy's attention turned to the parakeet, he slipped out of Guy's pocket on to the top of the cage, ran quickly to the side that was nearest the window and began climbing down the bars towards the window ledge. The guinea pigs regarded him with sleepy astonishment.

'Look at the budgies, Jackie,' Guy said.

'Come on, you,' said Jackie. 'I thought you'd come here for hamster food. If you're not careful, you'll end up with a houseful of pets!'

'Well, don't let me stop you,' said Mr Wiggs, and they all laughed.

Meanwhile Frank ran past one tank after another in the huge window. He set a pack of little gerbils squeaking and running after him in one tank, and in another a long brown snake lifted its head and hissed. But where were the hamsters?

'No hamsters at the moment?' said Guy, and Jackie said, 'Don't tell me you want another hamster!'

'We've none in right now,' said Mr Wiggs. 'They all sold in the run-up to Christmas. Very popular at Christmas, hamsters. But I'm expecting another litter in next week.'

No hamsters! thought Frank. Now what was he supposed to do?

Mr Wiggs fastened the bags of hamster food and handed them over.

'I hope your hamsters are well,' he said, and Guy and Jackie both said that they were, and that they'd be back in again soon. Then the door jingled open, there was a cold blast of air, and they were gone.

'Now what?' Frank said to the voice.

But almost immediately the door opened again.

'Are you the proprietor?' a woman's voice said.

'That's right, ma'am – Mr Wiggs of Wiggs's Pet Shop. What can I do for you?'

Frank scampered to the end of the window sill and climbed up the side of a metal cage containing rabbits.

'Hamsters,' the man said, and Frank nearly fell off the cage trying to see them, because he was suddenly absolutely sure that these people were the reason he was here.

'Well, now, isn't that strange,' Mr Wiggs was saying. 'You're the second person asking about hamsters, and I've not long since opened the shop!'

'We want to buy them,' said the woman in

imperious tones. 'As many as you've got.'

From the top of the rabbit cage Frank could see the backs of the two people talking to Mr Wiggs. The woman wore a long, sweeping green coat and her hair was piled fantastically on top of her head. The man was shorter and bald.

'Well, but that's what I've just been saying,' said Mr Wiggs. 'I'm all out of hamsters – sold every one over Christmas.'

'Out of hamsters?' the woman said incredulously. 'This *is* a pet shop, I take it?'

'Indeed it is,' said Mr Wiggs, sounding a little indignant. 'And I've got other pets, as you can see. But no hamsters at the moment. I'm expecting some in any time.'

The man peered towards a cage in the far corner. 'What's that, then?' he said.

'That?' said Mr Wiggs, distracted. 'Oh, no, he's not for sale. He's more of a family pet.'

Chestnut! thought Frank, delighted to hear that his old friend was still there.

'Would you be at all interested in showing him?' the woman queried, leaning forward.

Mr Wiggs laughed. 'Showing Chestnut?' he said. 'I think you'll find he's a bit long in the tooth for all that. He barely wakes up these days.'

Frank knew he had to attract their attention. Above him there was a birdcage containing a small cockatoo who was asleep on his perch. For the second time that morning, Frank performed his Lightning Twist Propulsion Manoeuvre. He leapt upwards and grabbed the bars at the bottom of the cage. The cage swung violently and the cockatoo woke with a terrific, deafening squawk that almost made Frank let go of the bars.

Mr Wiggs and his customers wheeled round in alarm, then stared, astonished, at the small, acrobatic hamster dangling from the cockatoo cage.

'What on earth –?' said Mr Wiggs, pushing his glasses back up his nose.

'I thought you said you didn't have any hamsters,' said the man, and the woman said, 'Oh, catch him, Vernon, quick!'

Frank allowed himself to be caught in Vernon's

plump and rather sweaty hands. Vernon carried him carefully to the counter.

'Well I never,' said Mr Wiggs. 'Where did you come from?'

'Never mind that,' said the woman. 'He's a fine specimen. We'll take him.'

'How much?' said the man, flicking open his wallet.

'But he might belong to someone,' said Mr Wiggs. 'I don't know how he got here – he isn't mine.'

'Then you won't want any money for him,' replied Vernon, shutting his wallet again, and the woman scooped Frank up. Frank had the impression of long green fingernails closing round him like claws. *Green* fingernails? he thought, but she was already pressing him up against the collar of her coat and he was swamped by the overwhelming smells of perfume and animal fur.

'Now just hold on a minute –' Mr Wiggs began, but the woman ignored him.

'At least it wasn't a *total* waste of time coming here,' she said, as Vernon opened the door. 'We'll be back next week for the others.'

And she swept out, as Mr Wiggs spluttered indignantly, carrying Frank towards the neon green car.

Meanwhile, as Guy and Jackie approached home, they could hear loud rumbling and roaring noises, the grinding sounds of great machinery. They looked at one another and hurried round the corner on to Bright Street. There, on The Wild, was a forklift truck, and a huge yellow digging machine. Several men in overalls and hard yellow hats stood round. Jackie ran towards them, followed by Guy.

'What's going on?' she asked.

'Just cordoning off the area, love,' said a man with a clipboard and pen, who appeared to be the foreman.

'What for?'

'Haven't you read the notice?' he said.

'What notice?'

The foreman pointed to a lamp post on the far side of The Wild. Now that they looked, they could see that someone had stuck a tiny scrap of paper to it. Jackie and Guy hurried over.

PLANNING PERMISSION Number 233976 L, it read.

Notice is hereby given that planning permission has been granted for twenty-two town houses to be built on the stretch of land between Bright Street and Harper Street, Plot Number 75146X. Anyone wishing to view the Plans may do so at the Town Hall, ext. J . . .

'I don't believe it,' said Jackie.

'Twenty-two houses?' said Guy.

'There's never room for twenty-two houses on this plot of land,' he said to the foreman as they returned. The foreman shrugged.

'Don't ask me,' he said. 'I didn't make the Plans.'

'When did you put that notice up?' asked Jackie.

'Let me see,' he said, scratching the side of his head with a pencil. 'Could have been a Thursday. Or a Wednesday. Might have been a Tuesday – no – it's line dancing Tuesdays.' He looked up. 'Before Christmas, anyhow.'

'But none of us have been out over Christmas —'

'Ah,' said the foreman. 'That'll be why you haven't seen it, then,' and he turned to the man who was unwinding yards of orange tape from a big roll.

'Bit more over here, Al,' he shouted.

Jackie and Guy gazed at one another in dismay. 'We've got to see the Plans,' Jackie said, 'and put in our objections, quick.'

'It's a bit late for that, love,' the foreman said, turning back. 'Work starts tomorrow.'

'*Tomorrow?*' exclaimed Guy. 'You can't start tomorrow!' but the foreman shook his head sadly. 'It's like I always say,' he sighed, 'you and me, we're the little people, caught up in bigger things. Wheels of history turn and we're just clinging to the spokes.' Jackie and Guy stared at him as he wandered off, still shaking his head.

'I don't believe it!' Jackie said. 'I've been on at the council for ages to make a proper park for the kiddies.'

'There's never room for twenty-two houses,' Guy groaned. 'They'll have to stack them all on top of one another!'

'That councillor practically promised me — I've got a letter somewhere —'

'There wouldn't be room for any gardens — not even a backyard — and what about parking?'

Jackie stared after the foreman, then narrowed her eyes. 'They're ignoring me,' she said, then tugged Guy's arm. 'Come on, there's no time to lose. We've got to find those Plans and stop them!'

4 Enemy Territory

Frank had never travelled in a car before, and this car travelled at speed. Mrs Taylor dashed through lights just as they were turning to red and took corners as though she had learned to drive on a racetrack. Every time Frank tried to work out where they were going he was flung back against the perspex wall of his new cage or flattened against the sides. He could work out that they seemed to be leaving the town because gradually the noise of traffic and people lessened and the scents around him changed to the bare, lonely smells of winter. He could hear birds calling to one another from the leafless trees.

By the time the car finally screeched to a halt, Frank felt rather battered and sick. He was hoisted out by the same hands that had carried him from the pet shop, with their green, talon-like nails, and carried through the cold air towards a long, low building, partially screened by bushes and trees.

TAYLOR-MAID LABORATORIES, a sign over the door read, SCIENTIFICALLY IMPROVING YOUR PETS.

Frank wasn't at all sure that he liked the look of that,

but there was no time to change his mind, since Mrs Taylor was already unlocking the door.

Inside there was a flood of warmth and brightness, as Vernon switched all the lights on. Marcia put Frank's cage down on what seemed like a reception desk and followed Vernon through a door at the back. Frank peered round the room attempting, despite the glare of the fluorescent lights, to work out exactly where he was.

The room was painted pale green, and on the walls there were pictures of hamsters, but they were like no hamsters Frank had ever seen. He screwed his eyes up against the brightness and stared at the nearest one.

ANNABELLE, it said on a little plaque beneath the photograph. *1ST PRIZE WINNER, MADRID.*

Annabelle had long curling hair that looked more like a judge's wig than a hamster's pelt. It fell in great ringlets all around her and there was so much of it that Frank wondered how she ever moved. But it was not the length that had attracted his attention at first, so much as the fact that every last strand of it was a shimmering, luminous green.

Frank stared at the photograph, swallowing hard. It must be a trick of the light, he told himself, or a trick of the camera, perhaps. He made himself look at the other pictures, though these were further away.

RUPERT ST JOHN-LE VERT, another plaque read, and there was a picture of a large, golden brown hamster. Frank couldn't see anything unusual about him at first, but then he noticed that Rupert's pelt had some very unusual markings. It was dappled and striped, almost like the markings of a great cat, and the markings were a distinct shade of, yes, green.

Frank could hardly believe his eyes. What was going on here? But before he had time to thoroughly investigate, Vernon and Marcia returned.

'Compartment H should do nicely,' Marcia was saying, and Vernon followed with something like, 'I've adjusted the flow,' then he picked Frank's cage up and carried him through the door.

Immediately Frank's nose was assaulted by a great range of scents. There was the overwhelming scent of hamsters and other, more sickening smells: chemical, acidic, bleach and something that Frank had never smelled before, but recognized anyway, the sour smell of sickness and disease. It was a combination of smells that reminded Frank sharply of the Room Beneath, where Mad Vince had destroyed hamsters for their pelts; yet it was not the same.

The range of scents was the first thing that struck Frank, and the next was a low whirring hum, not unlike the hum of the great machine he had discovered in the substation on his last adventure, only nowhere near as loud. Over this was the whispering of many hamster voices, all talking at once so that Frank couldn't hear properly what was said. Finally, after his other senses had batted information at him almost too quickly to be taken in, Frank stared round.

The walls of the room were lined with small plastic units shaped like shoeboxes. These were lined with absorbent bedding and some cotton material for shredding and nesting. In each unit, as far as Frank could make out, there was a hamster, a bowl of food and a small plastic tube from which the whirring noise came and from which, Frank discovered as he was lowered into his unit, a flow of air blew like a small breeze.

'There you are, my beauty,' Vernon said as he put Frank down. 'You have a snack and a good sleep.'

Frank could hear murmurs and squeaks from all the other shoebox units. He could hardly wait for Vernon to go so that he could talk to some of the other hamsters and find out what was going on, but Vernon kept fussing with his food and with the air flow, and adjusting Frank's water bottle.

'I've added a few vitamins to the water,' he told Frank. 'A little cocktail of my own to set you up for the morning.' A plump finger prodded Frank, and Frank bared his teeth. 'Not that you need much building up,' Vernon went on. 'A fine specimen. Really quite remarkable . . .' He seemed likely to stand and chat to Frank all morning, but just then Marcia's voice came from the next room.

'Vernon? Are you ready to help me with the cytology tests?'

'Coming, angel,' Vernon trilled and he snapped the lid down on Frank's unit and hurried away. Almost immediately the chorus of whispers and squeaks began again, but with all the hamsters talking at once it was hard to hear anything other than a few phrases.

'It's starting again, it's starting again . . .'

'Oh, my poor head – I can't bear it . . .'

'Who's next, who will it be next?'

'Who'll be next for what?' said Frank, and immediately the babble died down. 'Well, come on,' he said. 'You were all chattering away before. What's going on – what is this place?'

'Well, well, well,' said a familiar voice. 'Might have known you'd show up. No show without Punch.'

Frank craned his head towards the corner of the room. 'Mabel?' he said. 'What are you doing here?'

'I'm having a good time,' Mabel said. 'Plenty of food, good temperature and lots of grooming.'

In a unit near Frank's, a hamster with a deep, bass voice gave a hollow laugh.

'Grooming,' he said bitterly. 'That's a good one.'

Frank turned to face the speaker and nearly fell over in surprise. It was the biggest hamster he had ever seen and he was a deep muddy-brown colour. But the real surprise was his ears, which flopped forward and down like the ears of a rabbit. Frank had to look twice to make sure that he really was looking at a hamster.

'I beg your pardon?' he said.

'Granted,' said the mud-brown hamster, then he returned to nibbling a carrot.

'Look,' said Frank. 'If there's something going on here, then I'd like to know what it is. I'm here to help.'

'Help,' said Mabel scornfully. 'Muck things up, you mean.'

The mud-brown hamster just went on munching.

'What do you mean about "grooming"?' Frank asked.

The mud-brown hamster barely lifted his head. 'Look around you,' he said.

Frank looked and tried to choke back his dismay. To one side of him there was a hamster with enormous pouches, which dragged behind him as he moved; directly facing him was a hamster with a hump on his back; and above was one with a long thick rudder like an otter's tail. The more Frank looked, the more he saw hamsters who were freakishly different: some with long ringlets, like the one he saw in the photograph, others with buck teeth like a rabbit. One had long incisors, and carefully implanted in each of them was an emerald that flashed and winked.

'I don't know what you call "grooming",' said the mud-brown hamster with the rabbit ears. 'I think "modifying" would be closer to it.'

Mabel snorted. 'Stuff and nonsense!' she said. 'These people just want to make the best of us so they can put us in for shows.'

'Shows?' said Frank. 'What shows?'

'Oh, they put us into shows all right,' said the mud brown hamster. 'They experiment on us until they have the most unusual design, then they show us and they win a lot of money.'

'You tell them, Mellor,' said a tiny hamster with three ears. 'Tell them what happens to the ones that don't win.'

'Some designs work better than others,' Mellor said, still chewing his food. 'Some don't come out right at all. Others are entered for shows, but they don't get anywhere. In either case the result is the same. They are taken through to that room there,' he nodded towards a closed door that Frank could only just see, 'and a different kind of gas is piped through this airflow here,' he nudged the pipe above him, 'and then it's a short, swift trip to the incinerator.'

Frank was so horrified that for a moment he couldn't speak.

'Haven't you – haven't you tried to – do anything?' he said at last.

Mellor went on chewing his carrot. 'What do you suggest?' he said.

Frank was astonished. 'Well, surely you've tried to

get out – to run away?'

Mellor only snorted in response, but the little hamster said, 'We've all tried to get out at one time or another. These aren't ordinary cages, you know. Try it for yourself.'

Frank did not need telling. He was already climbing up the pipeline towards the ceiling of the plastic unit. He nosed along it as far as he could to try to work out how it was fastened down, but as far as he could tell it was sealed all the way along the edge.

'See?' said the tiny hamster. 'We've all tried. First thing you do when you get here. Some of us try longer and harder than others, but in the end, we all give up. My name's Lugs, by the way,' he added.

Frank couldn't believe that they had all given up. 'What about when they come and feed you?' he asked. 'Or clean the units?'

'Well, they're pretty careful,' Lugs said. 'One of them always holds you while the other changes the food. Or they put you into one of the empty units over there.'

'On the rare occasions when some poor animal has escaped,' Mellor put in, 'he has lived to regret it. Look at Bryn, over there.'

Frank looked, and felt a shudder travel along his spine. Bryn was grey and scaly with a long, sweeping snout. As Frank looked at him in horror he gave a sad, honking squeak. Frank dropped to the floor of his unit.

'This is terrible,' he said. 'I can't believe you're all just sitting around waiting for them to experiment on you – I mean – how do they do it anyway? Do they operate?'

'Operate, inject, implant,' Mellor said, still chewing. 'Basically, they do what they want. Who's going to stop them? And even if we were to escape,' he said, rolling an eye in Frank's direction for the first time. 'Do you have any suggestions as to where we might go? Who might want a troop of diseased or mutilated rodents? Any suggestions?'

'Yes, as a matter of fact,' Frank said. He was thinking of George's new colony in The Wild, but Mabel laughed scornfully.

'He's about to tell you that you can all live wild and free,' she said. 'The way hamsters used to live – you know, hunt your own food, fight your own predators –'

'You don't think that's better than being experimented on?' Frank interrupted.

Mabel preened herself. 'Oh, I don't think they'll experiment on me,' she said. 'They're only trying to improve some of the rougher-looking ones. I don't *need* improvement,' she said, licking along the length of her forearm. 'Only this morning the woman told me that she couldn't improve on my dazzling pelt.'

'She might want to make it glow in the dark though,' said Mellor. 'That's what happened to that lot there.' He nodded towards a row of white hamsters on the far wall, who all looked quite ordinary, but terribly apathetic.

'It's the radiation sickness,' Lugs whispered. 'It gets to them in the end.'

'Listen to you all, moan, moan, moan,' Mabel said. 'None of you have got any ambition.'

'Shut up, Mabel,' said Frank. He was trying to think, but the only clear thought in his mind was, what had he got himself into now?

5 A New Threat

Winter in The Wild was a new and strange experience. First the ground had been damp and muddy for weeks as rain churned the surface. Worms wriggled deeper away from the rain and slugs lay on the overturned earth. Then the temperatures dropped, the ground hardened and cracked and the foliage disappeared. Ice extended into the openings of burrows, and on one of his forays to the surface, George found a frozen shrew near the entrance of his burrow. The earth felt different, all its energy drawn in and stored in the roots of plants rather than the leaves, and in the long nights, the black sky with its glittering pinpoints seemed to hang very low, closer somehow than in summer.

Well below, in the Great Chamber, the hamsters, shrews, voles and field mice huddled together. Here, at least, the frost couldn't touch them and lots of insects and beetles had buried their grubs deep so that they could be found and eaten. One or two of the bolder hamsters still went out foraging for berries, but most stayed below ground, helping to extend the new territory as far across The Wild as possible. More and more rodents abandoned their burrows and came into the Great Chamber as temperatures dropped, hoping to keep warm enough to stay alive during the long winter nights.

Even George, who slept at one end of the Great Chamber with Daisy and the cubs, was worried. He had never properly experienced a winter before and didn't know how long it might go on, or how cold it might get. Would there be enough grubs to see them all through? Daisy was about to have another litter of cubs, so very soon there would be more mouths to feed. Undoubtedly, this was their greatest test yet since coming to The Wild, but mainly what he felt in response to it was sleepy: a creeping sleepiness that came over him unexpectedly when he was overseeing the building or washing one of the cubs. He had never before experienced so powerful an urge to sleep. He woke less and less frequently, and stayed, most of the time, in a huddle with Daisy, Donal, Declan, Dermot, Danny, Dean and little Elsie.

Then one morning he was wakened by a terrific grinding and quaking noise. The pillars of the Great Chamber shook, and rubble fell on to the sleeping rodents who started awake in alarm. A babble of nervous voices rose.

'What is it?'

'What's happening?'

'Is it an earthquake?'

George didn't know what was happening, but the next moment it happened again, and there was a general scurry away from the farthest side of the Great Chamber, where the walls were shaking. George kept a tight hold of little Elsie and spoke sharply to Donal, who wanted to investigate. Daisy clung to the others.

The third time it happened there was a fall of earth at the far end of the Great Chamber, and another chorus of anxious voices.

'My burrow, my burrow!'

'We'll all be trapped!'

'What do you think, Boss?' said a voice close to George's ear. 'Shall we go up to see what's going on?'

It was Capper, the friendly field mouse who had helped George and Daisy when they first came into The Wild. At his side was Boris, one of the hamsters who had escaped with Frank from the electricity substation in Frank's last adventure.

'You can't go, Georgie,' said Daisy fearfully.

'Someone has to,' said Boris.

George felt that he needed to know the exact nature of the danger and that he couldn't just let Capper and Boris put themselves at risk. Besides, if the truth was known, he had begun to feel a little, well, trapped, in recent weeks.

'I won't be long,' he said to Daisy.

'Can we come too, Dad?' cried Donal, Declan, Dermot, Danny and Dean.

Daisy gave him a reproachful look as if to say, 'Now look what you've started.'

'Your place is with your family,' she said to him. She had been quite nervous lately, now that the cubs were due. George knew that there was no point arguing with her, but he also knew what he had to do. He reached over and kissed her briefly.

'I won't take any risks,' he said. 'And I'll be back as soon as I can. Cubs, look after your mother.'

'Awww, Dad!' said Dermot, Declan, Donal, Danny and Dean in unison, but George ignored them and turned to face Capper and Boris. 'Let's go,' he said.

Up and up they tunnelled until the soft earth hardened and was riddled with frozen runnels of water. George could see his breath coming out in a little cloud before him. He knew instinctively that his body wasn't ready to cope with this kind of temperature. He wondered if it was the teenage gangs again, playing terrible games with fireworks, and what he could do if it was. He found himself thinking of Frank, and wondering if he knew what was going on.

The thunderous rumbling and grinding noises grew louder as they reached the surface and there was a range of new smells: metallic and oily. When George finally poked his quivering nose out of the tunnel, it was met by a hail of sharp little stones, and he retreated again quickly.

'What is it, Boss?' said Boris from behind, and Capper said, 'Hold up, let me have a look.' And he squeezed past George to the surface. A moment later they heard him muttering, 'Oh, lor,' and 'Cripes!'

'What is it?' said George irritably, because Capper's hind paws were digging into his shoulder. Capper turned round and hissed sharply, 'Here, both of you – take a look at this!'

Hurriedly George and Boris joined Capper at the surface, then stood gaping at the huge yellow and orange machinery, the men in fluorescent jackets and hard hats and the steel bars and tape cordoning off The Wild. George watched open-mouthed as an enormous yellow digger swung creaking into life, bending its great jointed neck towards the earth.

'Oh, what is it?' he whispered, and Capper said, 'It's builders, that's what it is – come to take over The Wild,' and he told them both the story of some field mice he knew who had all had to evacuate a field when a new estate was built.

'None of their homes survived,' he said. 'There was nothing left, nothing at all. We might as well give up now and get out while we still can. There's no hope for the new territory – none at all!'

Meanwhile, Jackie had called a meeting of all the neighbours in her front room. Everyone was there, except for Tania's parents. Mrs Wheeler said that if there were going to be new houses, it would probably be an improvement. But Les and Angie were there, from number 3, and Arthur and Jean from number 9, and Mrs Timms, who was still living in number 1 while work was being done on her own house after the fire. She looked a different woman in a new purple dress, embroidered at the collar and cuffs, beaming at her newly discovered friends. Mr Marusiak, who owned number 1 Bright Street, wasn't there. He was visiting a friend in Germany, but he had written to her every day. All the children were there, except for Tania, and each of them had a glass of orange juice and a biscuit. Guy brewed cups of tea for the adults while Jackie passed round photocopies of the proposed Plans and wrote important headings on to a flip chart.

'If you ask me it's a bit too late,' said Arthur. 'They've already started!'

'They can always stop,' said Jackie. 'And that's what we're here to discuss.' She turned the first page of the flip chart. *POPULAR SUPPORT,* it said. 'Now – I've leafleted all the surrounding streets and I've got a petition together for the council. They know I've been campaigning for ages to get that land turned into a proper little park for the children. One councillor as good as promised me that it was happening.' She turned to the second page. *PUBLICITY,* it said. 'I've phoned the press and the local radio, and that might hold them up for a while – at least while we look into . . .' she pointed to the next heading, *'GROUNDS FOR OPPOSITION* – that's where Guy comes in. Tell us, Guy.'

Guy stood up looking rather nervous.

'Well, it's not good news, I'm afraid,' he began. 'We don't have a right to object to losing a view, or other things, like water pressure from the plumbing – that's been looked into – loss of light – they've checked all that. I'm afraid the council weren't very helpful –'

'Better to have new houses there than gangs of teenagers,' Arthur put in unhelpfully and Jean nudged him. Mrs Timms leaned forward. 'What about land for my kitties?' she said.

Arthur snorted, but Guy said, 'No, she does have a point there. The only thing that would make a difference, according to the council, would be if we could prove that the wildlife was being materially damaged – birds and frogs and so on.'

'Well, that's it then,' said Jackie, but Guy shook his head. 'They did say we'd have to *prove* it,' he said, 'and that's not easy. The best thing would be if there was some kind of endangered species out there. Then we'd only have to prove that it was its natural habitat. They gave me a number to ring and a man from the Countryside Agency's going to send me a list.'

There was a pause as everyone tried hard to think what kind of animal on the little stretch of waste ground might be an endangered species.

'Well, it's something, anyway,' Jackie said when no one came up with anything else. 'We can all scour the waste ground when the machines aren't at work – you kiddies can help too. We'll take the torches out and have search parties at night!'

'YEAH!' said Jake, Josh, Thomas and Lucy.

'I'm not leaving the new territory,' said George. 'No way!' Then they all flattened themselves as the drilling started. Upright lengths of wood were sunk into the ground, and huge scoops of earth were lifted out of it and dumped elsewhere.

'We've no choice,' said Capper sadly when there was a break in the drilling. 'Lose our new home, or lose our lives.'

'But how are we going to find anywhere else?' said George, and Capper shook his head.

'I knew it was all too good to be true,' said Boris.

George stared at the great machines. At least they weren't drilling directly above the Great Chamber –

not yet, at any rate. He wondered why Frank hadn't told them anything about it. Wasn't that one of the reasons why he'd decided to stay with the humans, so that he could warn the colony in The Wild if anything was happening? Still, warned or not, George didn't see that there was anything he could do except move. But where could they go?

Capper and Boris were staring at him expectantly, as if he had the answer, when the drilling noise began again, so that he could hardly think. He closed his eyes.

'Look,' he said. 'I'm not giving up just yet. New territories don't just fall from the sky. We – we have to go back and warn the others – and if any of them wants to leave, they can.'

'But, Boss,' began Boris, 'it's dangerous. We've got to get them all out.'

'We'll take that decision when we get there,' snapped George. He was worried because he really couldn't think what to do, and all the drilling was giving him a headache. He hoped, desperately, that he would be able to come up with a plan on the way back. Right now, surrounded by all this noise and chaos, he felt very alone. What would Frank do? he thought, but he couldn't clear his mind long enough to come up with an answer.

The three hamsters turned and ran back along the tunnel, each preoccupied with thoughts of danger. George knew he would have to address everyone in the Great Chamber and he tried to work out what he would say. All he could really think about was Daisy and the cubs, and the new litter expected any moment, but he had to think about everyone's welfare, not just his own family. How could he tell so many animals that the refuge they had built was about to be destroyed? That they were likely to be homeless? That they would have to run where they could and, instead of all working together, it would be every rodent for himself?

The tunnel twisted and turned, then plunged steeply downhill. Boris, Capper and George slid down the last few inches to the Great Chamber, where they were immediately surrounded by worried hamsters, shrews and mice.

'Did you see?'

'What's going on up there?'

'Are you all right, Georgie?'

George couldn't utter a word, but Boris spoke loudly.

'Back off,' he said. 'Give the Boss some space. He's got something he wants to say.'

There was a shuffling noise as all the creatures cleared a little space around George. Several pairs of eyes glowed at him in the darkness. George gazed in despair at all the eager faces. How could he destroy their hope? Once again he wished very much that Frank was there, that he didn't have it all to do himself. It was lonely being a leader, he thought.

There was some coughing and shuffling in the ranks, and Capper gave George a nudging look. George cleared his throat, then he cleared it again.

'Fellow rodents,' he began, slightly huskily. 'There is danger –' But hardly had he begun to speak when

there was a great grinding, rumbling, tearing noise, and
the whole of the Great Chamber seemed to shift.
George was flung sideways as the ground beneath him
shook and several creatures squeaked aloud in terror.
There was a further rumbling noise and the sound of a
great fall of earth. A wail rose from the back of the
Great Chamber.

'The roof's falling in!' cried several rodents. 'We're
trapped!'

6 Strange Meeting

'All right,' Frank said to the voice inside him. 'You got me here – now how do I get out?'

Nothing.

Frank sighed deeply and tried again. All was quiet in the green room, except for the soft whirring of the air conditioning. Several hamsters seemed to have fallen asleep. Moments ago Vernon had come in and closed the green blinds so that the room was now shady and cool, and at the back the white hamsters that Mellor had pointed out before were glowing eerily in the green shade.

Frank couldn't get over the resignation and apathy in the room. None of these hamsters seemed to want to avoid their fate. There was an odour of fear, but it was a stale fear, trapped somehow, as if nothing could be done. Frank felt profoundly affected by the sense of hopelessness and dread. He felt as if he had wandered into a nightmare. He struggled against this feeling and tried to concentrate.

'Frank,' hissed a voice. Frank jumped and looked round. It was Mabel. Frank ignored her and tried to think again of a course of action.

'Frank!' Mabel hissed.

'What is it?' said Frank irritably.

'Have you thought of a plan yet — for getting us out?'

Frank stared. 'I thought you didn't want to get out,' he replied.

'Don't be silly,' snapped Mabel. 'Of course I do!'

'But you said —'

'That was *before*!' said Mabel. She sounded truly worried. 'I never said I wanted to be operated on, did I? I mean — look at this lot! They're all freaks!'

Mabel was on the back row with the other white hamsters, all of whom were glowing green.

'Oh, I see,' said Frank. 'It's finally occurred to you that you might be in trouble as well.'

'Don't be clever,' Mabel snapped. 'Just — just think of a way of getting us out of here.'

Getting you out, you mean, Frank thought, but all he said was, 'That's what I'm trying to do. I just need to think.'

A moment passed, then, 'Frank!'

'*What?*'

'Have you thought yet?'

Frank opened his mouth to give Mabel the sharp end of his tongue, when suddenly the door opened and they both froze. A monstrous apparition entered the room. It was like nothing Frank or Mabel had ever seen before. If anything, it looked like something Frank had once seen on Guy's TV, in a programme about astronauts. It had a huge deformed head with a glass mask in front, swathes of surgical clothing and big, clumping boots. Its breath made a loud sucking and hissing noise as it approached.

Frank could hear Mabel whimpering in fear and felt his own fur standing on end. The big clumping boots passed Mabel.

Mellor opened a bleary eye. 'It's only Vernon,' he said. 'Time for someone to go into the treatment room.'

The monstrous shape hissed and sucked and flapped and clumped its way towards the shelves on which Frank's unit was stacked. It was coming for Frank!

'Ah,' said Mellor sadly. 'It's your turn.'

Frank scurried frantically around his unit, but there was nowhere to hide. He felt a deep, uncontrollable horror welling inside. 'I suppose this is your idea of getting me out,' he said to the voice inside. 'Well, thanks a bunch!'

The sucking and hissing noise filled his ears as the monstrous form approached. Frank flattened himself against the back of his unit, then forced himself to look. Through the glass visor he could dimly see the outline of Vernon's eyes as gloved fingers prised open the front of Frank's unit.

This is it! Frank thought. His chance to make a run for it. But no sooner had he tensed all his muscles for his Lightning Twist Propulsion Manoeuvre than the gloved fingers were around him, prising him away from the back wall of the unit.

Frank kicked and wriggled and tried to bite, but the gloved fingers were impenetrable.

'Come on out, little hamster,' Vernon sang to him in

a voice horribly distorted by the mask. 'Nowhere to run, nowhere to hide,' and he lifted Frank out of the perspex unit and carried him, clump, clump, clump, towards the closed door at the far end of the room.

Frank could feel himself sweating in horror. He had the brief impression of many pairs of eyes following him mournfully as he left the room. 'Think, think!' he told himself, and he stopped struggling. Now was the time to call on his other powers.

The problem was that Frank was more frightened than he had ever been in the whole of his life. The other times he had faced danger, with the rats in the sewers, or mad humming Humphrey in the substation, or even Vince who had wanted to flay hamsters for their pelts, it had been the kind of danger he could understand to some extent, and cope with. But this – the threat of being kept powerless in a laboratory and experimented on – represented his worst, most nightmarish fears. A sense of horror almost paralysed him now. Yet somehow he had to clear his mind and focus on what he needed to do. He had to summon the power that he had called on before.

The door swung shut behind them. 'Help me!' Frank called inwardly and even in his own mind it sounded like a terrified squeak. 'Help!'

In the centre of Frank's mind a blackness grew, that might have been the blackness of unconsciousness, or it might have been, as Frank desperately hoped it was, the Black Hamster of Narkiz.

'Please!' he begged it. 'Please, please come now.'

In the past, the Black Hamster had always come

when Frank needed him, but now nothing happened. In the depths of his mind Frank called him, with every ounce of his strength, but no Black Hamster appeared. Instead, the voice came.

'Use the power,' it said.

Frank was almost too numb with panic to understand, yet he suddenly had a clear memory of the time when he had made Vince do what he wanted by communicating directly with his mind. Now, as the great flapping, sucking thing that was Vernon carried him across to a special unit, Frank stopped trying to summon the Black Hamster and instead tried to sink into the darkness in the centre of his mind. At first he couldn't do it, then he realized he was trying too hard. It was more a kind of *allowing*. Inwardly, he stepped back into a darkness that was surrounded by a silvery light. He could feel a thread of light connecting him to the creature that was Vernon.

'Stop now,' he thought, from the centre of the darkness. 'Put me down.'

And Vernon stopped. In the middle of the room he stood still, as though confused. Frank knew that he mustn't give in to panic; he had to stay in the centre of the dark place. 'Put me down,' he said, and he knew he was speaking directly into Vernon's mind.

The fingers round Frank opened and he dropped on to a wooden bench. Immediately he was gripped by the impulse to run, but no sooner had he given in to this impulse, than he left the dark, safe place and he heard Vernon's voice shouting, '*Hoy!*'

Frank ran. He darted round or behind the objects on

the bench, and there were lots of them: test tubes, thermometers, Bunsen burners, little glass phials that spun off the edge of the bench and shattered on the floor, tweezers and finally a bottle of foul-smelling chemical that broke and sent Vernon into a coughing fit as he followed Frank.

This was just the chance that Frank needed. Overpowered by the fumes that penetrated even his protective clothing, Vernon doubled over, coughing and spluttering, while Frank ran along pipes that led away from the bench, along the wall and to another bench. All he could think of was getting away. The fumes were scorching the back of his own throat, but at least he was running away from them, whereas Vernon had been enveloped by a sharp blast and was now blundering his way along the bench, knocking

things over, unable to see Frank for the tears in his eyes.

'If I ever get away from here,' Frank said to the voice in his mind as he pelted along, 'I'm not coming back, even for the others. No way.'

The second bench contained plastic units like the ones in which Frank and the rest of the hamsters had been kept, but these were attached to large bulbous tubes that contained things that Frank would rather not see: small rodent-like organisms suspended in liquid, opening and closing their mouths like fish, while in the main unit, a hamster lay on its side as if paralysed. Frank's mind revolted and he looked away.

'I can't rescue them all, do you hear me?' he said to the voice within. 'They'll have to look out for themselves. I've got to save my own skin!'

And as Vernon staggered to the windows and doors,

opening them all to get rid of the scorching fumes, Frank hardened his heart to the pitiful sights in the perspex units as he scampered past. For once he was going to look after himself. This was the worst thing he had ever faced and it was too much for one hamster to take on. He had never run away before, and he was sorry to do it now, but there came a time when you had to admit defeat. He wasn't the saviour of the entire hamster race, he was one small hamster, struggling alone, desperately trying to survive.

Then, as he was passing the last perspex unit, something made him turn around. Perhaps it was a scent of something old and so familiar, closer to him than his own blood. Without wanting to, he stopped and stared.

There in the perspex unit was a silky grey hamster, lying on her side with her eyes closed. The long, fluffy fur had an almost lilac sheen. Frank would have known her anywhere, though in fact he had only seen her twice since being taken from her as a tiny cub: once in a shared memory with Chestnut, and once in a vision with Humphrey. The last time he had had a vision of Narkiz, he had been told that he would see her again when the time was right, and now here she was in this terrible place, the one hamster he felt he had been looking for all his life: his mother, his dam.

'Leila,' he breathed, and suddenly oblivious to Vernon, who had pulled off his headgear in an attempt to breathe and was now advancing again towards the benches, Frank pressed both paws up against the perspex container.

'Leila,' he said again, and the sleeping hamster stirred. Something quivered along the length of Frank's spine — hope, love, desire, fear? Whatever it was, he pushed both paws hard against the perspex and called her name again, 'Leila!'

And Leila opened her eyes.

7 Hope

'Everyone out!' shouted Boris and Capper, while George grabbed hold of Daisy and ushered the cubs along. 'Come on – move along! This way – quick!'

There was another rumbling crash as more of the ceiling fell in at the far end of the burrow. One strand of a tangled root broke free and bobbed about wildly, and everywhere there were cries of 'Help, help!'

Boris and Capper and one or two rats worked furiously to free some of the smaller rodents who were trapped in the falling earth. Fortunately, the earth, having been turned over, was soft and crumbling and it wasn't too hard to dig them out. Once released, they ran furiously after the others, along the passages leading away from the Great Chamber.

George got Daisy into the nearest burrow and she sank down thankfully. He looked at her anxiously. 'Is it time?' he asked, but she shook her head.

'Nearly though,' she said. 'Are all the cubs here?'

George looked round swiftly. Donal, Dermot, Declan, Danny and Dean were clustered round, but where was little Elsie?

'Here I am!' said Elsie, appearing suddenly from a

side entrance. Her coat was covered in fallen earth, but she was smiling. 'Willow got himself stuck, but he's all right now.' Willow was a shrew and her special friend.

'You've got no right disappearing like that,' Daisy said crossly. 'I – Oh!'

'Mum's having the babies,' Donal said, and little Elsie hurried over.

'I am not!' said Daisy. 'Where's your father?'

'Here,' said George, returning. 'Daisy – I don't know what to do –'

But before he could say any more, Boris and Capper and a rat called Tucker appeared at the entrance to the burrow.

'Everyone's out, Boss,' Boris said, 'and no one's hurt.'

'Oh, good,' both George and Daisy said thankfully.

'They're all waiting to hear from you,' Capper said. 'Looks like only part of the ceiling's collapsed. We could try going back, if you like.'

Everyone looked at George, and he licked his lips. It was true that all the horrible noises had stopped, but was it safe? But if they didn't go back, would that be the end of the New Narkiz?

Not for the first time that day, George wished that Frank was with him. But he had to say something now.

'Well,' he began. 'What are the options?'

'Substation,' Boris said promptly. 'You know – where we all lived before Frank came. "S'perfectly safe.'

George thought. The substation had the advantage of being immediately close to their territory. From there they would be able to see when the danger was over. On the other hand, it was possible that the substation was under threat too and would be destroyed along with the rest of The Wild.

'There's the sewers,' Capper said. 'I've been in them many a time. There's loads of room.'

George had been in the sewers too, of course, and he hadn't thought much of them. Nasty, dank smelly places, subject to sudden floods. And there were packs of rats, who had attacked them on one occasion. But what choice was there? George thought hard, and everyone looked at him.

'We don't really know,' he said, 'which bits of The Wild are under threat, and which are safe. Same with these other places – the substation and the sewers – they might be under attack too. Or it might all be over now – we might all be safe. So what I propose is this. Most of us should stay here and start to build new burrows, away from the big machines. But some of us should form scouting parties and go and look for new, safe places – on the other side of The Wild, or in the substation, or down the sewers. We need some volunteers –'

'Me! Me! Me! Me! Me! Me!' shouted Donal, Dermot, Declan, Danny, Dean and little Elsie, and Daisy said, 'You can't all go! And *you're* not going at all, little Elsie. I need you here with me.'

'That's not *fair*!' shouted little Elsie. 'I always get to do the boring stuff!'

George raised his paws. 'You can't all come,' he said. 'We need to carry on building away from the Threat, and to keep a lookout, to see if we can work out which way it's coming, so we know where to build. I have to be here for Daisy,' he said, and everyone nodded. Daisy squeezed his paw. 'But we need two small scout parties – one for the substation and one for the sewers.'

'Me! Me! Me!' cried all the cubs again, but George said, 'Danny, Declan, Dean, I need you with me to do the building work and keep a lookout.'

'Yes, Dad,' said Danny, Declan and Dean, in a resigned kind of way.

'Little Elsie stays with her mum, that goes without saying.'

'*Awww!*' cried little Elsie, but George ignored her and went on firmly, 'Boris, you know the substation. You can take one or two of the others who came from there with you, and maybe Dermot here.'

Dermot grinned in delight.

'Check out the territory, see if it's under threat, how many might safely move there, that kind of thing. Capper – you've been to the sewers before, but you need a rat with you in case you meet any others – so take Tucker with you, and maybe one other – and – yes – Donal.'

Donal swelled with pride and he and Dermot smacked one another's paws while Declan, Danny and Dean looked on resentfully. But this was George's way of demonstrating that he would include his own family in any dangerous undertaking, without putting all of them at risk. Besides, Donal and Dermot were the eldest and needed to try their paws at new experiences.

'So that's decided, then,' said George, ignoring little Elsie, who was still muttering about boring babies, and it not being fair. It's the best I can do, he thought to himself.

Capper and Boris had already set off in their separate directions to round up one or two other volunteers, and Donal and Dermot were following excitedly when there was another rumpus from the Great Chamber.

'It's starting again, it's starting again!'

'Quick, get out before the whole thing falls!'

'Into the burrows, quick!'

George and his remaining sons hurried to see what was happening. Daisy struggled to get up, but sank back gasping, 'Oh, dear! Oh, dearie dear!'

Little Elsie hung back. She was still simmering with resentment at being given the role of Mum's helper. Because she was the smallest and the only girl, she was often treated very protectively by her parents and brothers, when really all she longed for was adventure. She was rarely allowed out foraging with the others, and if the burrow needed tidying, it was always, 'Oh, that's a job for little Elsie!' Well, she'd had just about enough of it. While the others hurried out of the burrow to see what was going on, little Elsie pretended to follow. But as soon as they reached the Great Chamber, under cover of the general confusion, she slipped away and darted into another burrow, which was the one she knew Capper used when he wanted to get away from The Wild altogether. Gathering speed, and without stopping to look to the right or left, little Elsie followed Capper, Tucker and her brother as they travelled towards the sewers.

8 Battle

It took Frank a moment or two to realize that, though Leila's eyes were open, she couldn't see him. There was a greenish tinge to them, as though they had been covered with a glaze. Leila was blind.

Frank smacked his paws repeatedly against the perspex container. 'Leila!' he cried in anguish. 'What have they done to you?'

Leila lifted her head in a slow, dazed motion. 'Wh–Who is it?' she said, and Frank was about to tell her, to say that it was her son, Frank, when Vernon's plump hand, devoid of glove, clamped round him. 'Gotcha!' he said.

But Frank felt a spark of rage flare in him and suddenly he was blazing mad. He bit into the tender part of Vernon's thumb, and when Vernon squawked and released him, he didn't run, but tensed all his muscles and sprang, landing full on Vernon's face and sinking his teeth into his nose.

Vernon howled with pain and fear and blundered round the room swatting madly at his face. Frank hardly even noticed the blows. He dug his claws and teeth in as never before. All he could think was that if there was a way of making these people pay for what they'd done, then he, Frank, was going to find it. All thoughts of running away were gone.

'What on earth's going on?'

It was Marcia in the doorway, gazing in astonishment at the sight of Vernon stumbling round the room with a hamster on the end of his nose. He pulled at Frank and Frank dropped from his nose to his lower lip, where he bit even harder.

'AAIOWW!' roared Vernon. 'Ongle gunky glik hamster!' and he tried desperately to tear Frank away from his lower lip, but Frank bit even harder, so that Vernon's lower lip stretched further and further away from the rest of his face.

'Let me try,' said Marcia, and she crossed the room in two strides and flicked Frank smartly on the nose with one of her long green fingernails. In a reflex action, Frank released his grip on Vernon's lip and fell into Marcia's hands, where he lay panting for a moment, tears stinging his eyes.

A moment was all it took for Marcia to have Frank sealed in an empty unit once more.

'Throw him in the incinerator!' howled Vernon. 'He's a savage beast!'

'Certainly not,' said Marcia, and she inspected Frank thoughtfully through the perspex unit. 'This one's a fighter.'

'A fighter?' cried Vernon, still mopping the blood from his nose and mouth. 'He's a raving lunatic!'

'Could be a champion though,' Marcia said, still gazing at Frank, who by this time had got up and was running round the sides of the perspex container, pressing them hard from time to time with his paws. 'I think we should try him on the steroid drip.'

Vernon stared. '*The steroid drip?*' he said incredulously. 'Take a raving lunatic and make him ten times stronger and even more mad?'

'Where's your imagination, Vernon?' Marcia said. 'One or two of these bigger boys would make for impressive gladiatorial displays.'

Vernon stopped mopping his face. 'Oh, I see,' he said in a changed voice.

'We could even train them to use weapons, ride chariots, the works . . .'

'Fight to the death,' cried Vernon. 'No mercy!'

'And the stage all lit in green,' said Marcia, 'gladiatorial green!' She rose and stretched. 'He'll have to do without food for a while, then when he's quite empty, we can start the drip — later this evening!' She smiled at Vernon as she left the room and he just about managed to smile back with his damaged mouth. Then he followed her out, shaking his fist at Frank as he left.

By this time Frank had worked out that he couldn't open the unit from the inside. There was a special kind of catch on the outside that he couldn't get to with his teeth. And the walls were entirely smooth. Worn out by his efforts, he slumped back on to the container floor.

Then suddenly, startling him, Leila spoke.

'Are — are you still here?' she said in a whispery, silvery voice. 'Did they take you away?'

Frank got to his feet. 'I'm still here, Mu— Leila,' he

said, almost forgetting himself and calling her 'Mum', when really it would be better to introduce this idea gradually. Leila was in the next unit along, looking about vaguely with her sightless eyes, apparently unable to get up. Frank could hardly bear to see her like this.

'What happened?' she asked him.

Frank told her briefly that he had leapt at Vernon and bitten his nose, and a small sound escaped her, like the weariest chuckle.

'Did you bite hard?' she asked.

'Not hard enough,' said Frank, and he heard the throaty, floaty sound again, then she sighed.

'You attacked them,' she said. 'Yes, we all do that at first. But it makes no difference in the end.'

Frank rested his cheek against the wall of his container. 'What happened to you?' he said, though he was almost afraid to ask.

'You really want to know?' said Leila, and she sighed again. 'I wasn't always like this.'

Frank almost said 'I know,' but he stopped himself in time.

'No,' she said. 'I used to belong to someone. I had an Owner.'

Leila's Owner had been an elderly lady called Maud. When Maud's son had moved abroad he had wanted to buy her a pet to keep her company. But she wasn't allowed to keep cats or dogs in the flat where she lived, and she didn't really like birds in cages, so when her son passed the window of Mr Wiggs's Pet Shop and saw Leila with her beautiful silky fur, he thought that she would be the perfect choice.

'I was nursing my cubs at the time,' said Leila sadly, and once again Frank wanted to call out, 'I know! I know!' but he stopped himself.

'They weren't very old,' Leila continued. 'Not old enough to lose their mother. But what choice do we hamsters have in such things? There were eight of them,' Leila said, 'and who knows what has become of any of them? Still,' she went on, 'I was bought and taken to this old lady, and she treated me well. She was lonely and appreciated the company. We were two lonely ladies together. I became quite fond of her in the end,' and Leila sighed again.

'What happened to her?' Frank asked huskily.

Maud had collapsed one day in the flat, and it had been quite a long time before anyone had found her. Leila had rattled the bars of her cage and squeaked every time someone had come to the door, but no one had heard, and in the end it had been Maud's neighbour Edith who had got worried and raised the alarm.

Maud had had a minor stroke. It was hoped that she would recover, but the doctor said that she couldn't possibly live on her own any more. She had to go into a Home for the Elderly, where no pets of any kind were allowed. So there remained the problem of what to do with Leila.

Edith couldn't take her, since she had a horror of rodents, and it was too complicated for Maud's son to take her out of the country, so it seemed quite likely that Leila would have to be taken to the Vet. Then suddenly, out of nowhere, came the knock on the door.

'And when they opened it, there was the Woman in Green,' said Leila, with a delicate, convulsive shudder. 'She wafted in, all perfume and fingernails, saying "I hear there is a prahblem," ' and Leila did such a good imitation of Marcia's voice that in spite of the horrible situation, Frank nearly laughed.

'And of course Maud's son said that they needed a home for a hamster, and he couldn't take me since he had to work abroad, and Edith couldn't take me because she hated rodents, and Marcia said, "Really? I *lahve* rodents!" She even offered to pay for me, and Maud's son said that he couldn't possibly accept any money, he was just grateful to her for taking me, and the next thing I knew she was picking up my cage and bringing me here. I didn't even get the chance to say goodbye to Maud. That was three months ago now, I think – it's hard to tell. One day is just like another in here.'

Three months! Frank thought, horrified. He licked his lips. 'Wh– what have they done to you?' He felt he had to know, though he didn't want to.

'It doesn't matter,' Leila said, and she put her head down as though she was too weary to talk any more.

'No – no really – I want to know. You – you can't see, can you?'

For a long moment Leila was quiet, then she said, 'No, I can't see. Sometimes I think it's probably better that way.' She told him what he already knew, that they were trying to make the perfect hamster for their shows. '*Designer* hamsters, they call us,' she said with just a touch of bitterness. Leila was already beautiful, and

Marcia thought she would be perfect for the shows, but then they had tried to give her emerald green eyes, like Marcia's own. When the experiment had failed and Leila had lost her sight, she had thought that they would simply destroy her like the others. But then Marcia had thought of a new experiment. They wanted to use tissues from Leila's body and mix them somehow with tissue samples from other, prize-winning hamsters, to grow their own, *improved* hamsters.

'That's what the creatures in the tubes are,' Leila said sadly. 'Thus far, none of them have survived. I'm just happy that I don't have to look at them.'

Frank felt overwhelmed by horror and disgust. He could see now that the pink blobs in the tubes were small, unformed hamsters at varying stages of development. He closed his eyes and ground his teeth in agony. He felt that he had never known, until now, the full depth of his rage and bitterness against humans, partly because he himself had been treated well by Guy. Yet he had lost his mother, he had been bought and sold into captivity, to live in a cage, like the rest of his race. And who knew what had happened to his other family? Without humans, hamsters would all be living wild and free in Syria, in the territory called Narkiz, not trapped in laboratories like this, where mad people performed unnatural experiments on them. There was no word big enough to describe what Frank felt for humans at that point. But somehow he managed to speak.

'You have suffered, Leila, you really have,' he said.

'But I'm here now, and as long as I live, I won't let them hurt you again.'

Leila lifted her head wonderingly at this and gazed in his direction with her beautiful, sightless eyes. 'You?' she said. 'But why? Who are you?' Frank opened his mouth to tell her but suddenly the door at the back opened again and Vernon entered, once more in his protective gear. He rapped on Frank's cage as he passed.

'Nearly time for you, big boy,' he said. 'Betcha can't wait!' and he giggled his stupid, high-pitched giggle. Frank bared his teeth. He felt a loathing so strong he was almost sure it could blast and destroy Vernon without Frank having to move, but Vernon carried on oblivious. He went to all the tubes containing the tiny, unformed hamsters and inspected them carefully, tutting and shaking his head.

'Oh, dear,' he muttered. 'Oh, dearie, dearie dear.' Then with sudden, brutal movements he snapped the tubes away from the containers, sealing the ends of the pipes that connected them with a clip and taking them all to a metallic hatch near the door. He opened this hatch and there was a sudden, dreadful reek.

'*Hasta la vista*, babies,' he said, then the hatch slammed shut again and there was the sound of tinkling glass. Frank stared in horror, and Leila raised her head.

'The incinerator,' she whispered. 'Another batch lost.'

Then Vernon returned to the units, checking that each had the right supply of food, drink and air. He flicked Frank's container again as he passed.

'No food for you, big boy,' he said, and winked. Frank felt himself shaking with rage, but he was suddenly alert as Vernon bent over Leila's unit.

'Time to go sleepy-bies,' he said, and Frank saw him fill a little container with fluid. The fluid ran along a tube into Leila's cage from where it passed, Frank saw with a jolt of alarm, directly into Leila's spine. Leila quivered convulsively as the fluid passed into her, then slowly, slowly closed her eyes.

Frank smacked his paws against the perspex once more. 'Leila!' he cried.

Leila's eyelids fluttered. 'So sleepy,' she mumbled, and lapsed into unconsciousness.

Vernon straightened, looking pleased with himself. 'That's all for now, folks!' he said cheerily. 'We'll try again tomorrow. Toodle-pip!' and he was gone.

'Leila!' Frank cried again, but Leila did not respond. Frank sank down on to all four paws. He hadn't even had a chance to tell her who he was. But one thing was for sure, he told himself, he wasn't going to leave until she did know; in fact he wasn't going to leave without her at all. They would never be separated again.

Frank sat back on his haunches and tried to think clearly. He was in a perspex container, and apparently he couldn't get out. A lot of other hamsters were trapped here, he didn't know how many. They couldn't get out either, unless Frank released them. The ones he had met so far were either too injured, drugged or despairing to try to escape. They obviously didn't believe they *could* escape or that if they did, they would have anywhere to go. Frank knew that George wouldn't turn them away if he took them to The Wild, but how was he going to get them there? As far as he remembered, the car journey from the pet shop hadn't taken too long, though he had been too busy rolling about in his container and trying not to be sick to tell. But this place was definitely outside the town – much further than Frank had ever been before. And however was he going to lead a crowd of damaged, mutant hamsters all the way back to the centre of the town, when he didn't know the way himself?

These were all good questions, but Frank did not have the answers. He stared ahead as the full awfulness of his situation hit him. It was a desperate plight. Only one thing was certain — that he had to act somehow, and act soon. But what could he do?

In his dismay Frank held on to one thought. The Black Hamster had always helped him before, whenever Frank couldn't help himself. If Frank could help himself, then obviously the Black Hamster expected him to get on with it, but when the chips were really down, he was always there. And this situation was certainly the worst, the most appalling one Frank had ever encountered. Surely now, if he called the Black Hamster, he would come?

Frank licked his lips. He had never summoned the Black Hamster before, at least, not successfully; he had always just been there somehow, mysteriously, when Frank really needed him. Well, Frank definitely needed him now, and he couldn't imagine why he wasn't already there. But since he wasn't, Frank would have to try to call him.

Frank closed his eyes. He remembered his breathing. He remembered the voice he had heard earlier that day and the sensation of black velvety darkness. A series of images flickered across his mind of the times when he had encountered the Black Hamster before and seen Narkiz, so that even in this predicament, Frank couldn't help but smile. He remembered when the Black Hamster had appeared in terrifying, huge form to Vince, the madman intent on flaying hamsters for their skins, and he smiled even more, then reminded himself to get on with it. He let his mind sink into the centre of that darkness, and the darkness grew. Somewhere far above him, he felt sure there was a star.

And then, in the centre of the darkness, he was there. Frank couldn't see him, but he felt surrounded by him; by the presence of that dark, velvety intelligence. And as always he felt the sensation of joy welling inside him so that he almost forgot what he had to do. Then he spoke to the Black Hamster from the centre of his mind.

'Come to me,' he said, and he put into his request all his knowledge of the horror of the situation he was faced with, the need of the imprisoned hamsters and their terrible fate if he didn't rescue them. He added a full acknowledgement of his own helplessness; this was the worst evil he had ever faced, and he couldn't handle it alone. 'Help me, please,' he begged, and he waited as if for an eternity, for the answer.

There was a long pause in which Frank felt suspended like those poor unformed hamsters suspended in their tubes. He hung on, focusing his mind to a single point, until finally the answer came.

The answer was 'No.'

9 A Tale of Two Elsies

Elsie stood shivering on the pavement outside number 3 Bright Street. The last time she had left her house she had been captured by cats, so venturing outside now was the bravest thing she had ever done. But she was determined to find George. She needed to tell him what Lucy had told her, that if humans could find an unusual or endangered species in The Wild, the building work would have to stop. She had worried about the problem all night, and that morning an idea had come to her. She was going to try to persuade George to let the humans find the hamster colony, so that they might be able to save The Wild.

The air was damp and stank of petrol, and Elsie was freezing, but at least she couldn't smell cats. There was a huge puddle where the pavement met the road, and Elsie worried that she might have to try to swim it. She was edging her way along the kerb, trying to work out by sniffing whether the water ended at any point, when the car came. Before she could hear it, Elsie felt the vibrations through her paws, then almost instantaneously she heard the trembling roar, increasing in volume to an unbearable pitch. The pavement shook and Elsie flattened herself against it. The car tore through the puddle, sending a wing of water up from its wheels. The murky, freezing water descended in a perfect arc all over Elsie, who gasped in shock and then struggled to breathe. The water was muddy and reeked of petrol. Elsie shook herself violently, and a shower of tiny droplets flew from her pelt. She felt absolutely miserable, lonely and afraid, and soaking wet. 'Oh, well,' she told herself grimly. 'Whatever happens next, I can't very well get any wetter, or colder. I'll just have to take my chances with the cars.' And she took a deep breath and plunged into the freezing puddle.

Meanwhile, little Elsie, still following Capper and Tucker, had made her way into the sewer. She didn't like it much – it was cold, dank, smelly and dripping. Worst of all were the noises. The tunnels echoed and each drip of water sounded like an enormous plop. The dim roar of cars set up a rumbling vibration through the pipes and caused all the drops of water to drip at once in little showers. Like her aunty, little Elsie was wetter and colder than she had ever been in her life. She was also starving and getting tired. In The Wild she would have trapped a few beetles and grubs by now, but here there was nothing but filthy garbage, swirling round her paws.

She could still faintly hear noise ahead from Capper and Tucker and Donal, but the echoes magnified it, and each time she ran after them, they were not where she thought they were. So she was getting very dispirited, and beginning to wish that she had done as she was told in the first place. She thought guiltily of her mother, who might already be having the babies, and whom she, little Elsie, had left alone. She would really be in trouble when she went back. If she ever got back. Little Elsie was no longer sure that she could find the way home. If she didn't find the others soon she might be lost in these tunnels forever.

Thinking this caused a tear to quiver along little Elsie's nose and drop from the end of her whiskers with a tiny plop, echoing the bigger plops all around her. Suddenly she knew that it was time to give up her game of following the others and attract their attention, somehow, anyhow, before the noises ahead disappeared entirely and she was lost. Despite her fear of the echoes, and of the strange things that might lurk in the little tunnels leading off from the main one, little Elsie lifted her voice and squeaked aloud, 'Capper! Tucker! Donal!'

Then she flattened herself against the wall, deafened by the reverberating noise. 'Well, anyway, they must have heard that,' she told herself. '*Someone* must have heard.'

Someone had. Quite a few different someones, in fact. They came swarming out of the minor tunnels to the right and left, some running along the sides of the tunnels, some apparently along the ceilings. In no time at all they had surrounded little Elsie, dropping to the floor of the pipe. Elsie could hardly believe that there were so many of them, or that they could move so silently through the echoing maze.

The biggest of them reared in front of her to an

impressive size. His eyes glowed and his teeth were sharp and yellow.

'Well, well, well, chaps,' he said, licking his yellow teeth. 'What've we got here?'

Little Elsie wasn't automatically afraid of rats, since of course she had grown up with them in The Wild, but these seemed more hostile than any she had ever known. They were hunting, she knew that at once – they gave off the smell of the chase, and the kill. She knew that she was in more trouble than when she had thought she was merely lost, but she also knew that she mustn't panic. If she panicked and ran they would be on her in an instant.

Little Elsie did not lack courage. She drew herself up to her own full size, which was rather less impressive, and said, 'If you please, sir, I'm lost. I'm looking for a field mouse, a hamster and a rat. Have you seen them?'

'What – travelling together?' said one rat, but the biggest rat silenced him with a look.

'Suppose I had seen them?' he said, grinning, 'what's it to you?'

'I've got to find them,' cried little Elsie earnestly. 'Please tell me if you have!'

The biggest rat only grinned even harder. 'Come here,' he said to little Elsie. 'Come a bit closer.'

Little Elsie didn't want to go even the tiniest bit closer, but she didn't seem to have any choice. Glancing nervously at the surrounding rats, she took one step forward, then another.

'That's it,' said the biggest rat. 'Come to me.'

Little Elsie held her head high. She walked right up

to the biggest rat and stared at him without flinching.

'Would you look at that?' he said admiringly. 'Plucky little bint, ain't yer?'

He extended a long yellow paw and pushed her chin up further, further. His face was suddenly sharp and mean.

'Back off, lads,' he said to the surrounding rats. 'This one's for me!'

Hardly had the older Elsie struggled out of the puddle, dripping wet, when she felt the vibrations through her paws again, followed immediately by a distant roar. Another car! But she couldn't go back, or she might never cross the road. All her instincts told her to freeze and cower, but instead, she ran faster and faster, while the roaring increased to a terrible pitch. The other side of the road seemed miles away. Elsie's breath came in quick short spurts: faster, faster!

Then suddenly the car was upon her. Deafened, with the horrible stench of petrol and rubber filling her senses and a blast of heat lifting her pelt, Elsie flattened herself into the road. And the car drove over her, the wheels skimming past on either side!

Trembling all over, Elsie finally looked up. Her limbs felt as though they had turned to water, but she knew she had to get to the other side before another car came. She put one paw forward, then another, and trotted as fast as she could to the other side. It was like one of those dreams where you want to move fast, but instead seem to be going slower and slower. Yet somehow, impossibly, there she was, scrambling up the kerb to the pavement.

All was quiet, since the workmen were on their lunch break, and the big machines were at rest. But now she had reached the other side, Elsie couldn't stop running. She crossed the pavement swiftly and plunged into the wet grass, which rapidly became tangled and tall. Fronds of wet grass struck her face, making her sneeze. There were patches where she had to fight her way through, and patches where the grass suddenly cleared into bare earth, strewn with litter. There was an old shoe and a damp sock, and several bags of crisps, around which ants swarmed like a miniature army. Elsie nosed her way feverishly about, looking for the entrance to a burrow, any burrow. 'All the burrows lead to the Great Chamber sooner or later,' George had told her, and so she ran on through stones and litter and bracken, looking for any opening in the earth, her nose searching for the scent of hamster.

Suddenly, there was a rustling movement in the grass ahead, and the next moment a terrifying beast leapt out towards Elsie. It was a large spider, disturbed from its winter lair.

Elsie had never seen a spider this close, and it wasn't a pretty sight. She saw herself reflected in eight enormous eyes, its antennae quivered and its long, furred legs twitched. But it seemed to decide that Elsie was too big for food and leapt off suddenly on its silken thread.

Elsie stayed where she was for a moment. Her heart was beating so rapidly that she could hardly move. Then slowly she moved away from the long grass, further into the clearing. Miserably, she acknowledged to herself that she didn't know where to look, that she might very well be lost. A sense of hopelessness overcame her. Why had she ever left her nice warm cage?

A moment or two later, telling herself that she couldn't very well stay where she was, Elsie set off again, much more slowly. She made herself look thoroughly and systematically beneath the bracken for any holes, or any signs of hamster activity, such as paw prints or droppings.

At last she was rewarded by the faintest of scents. It came from beneath a clump of nettles. Elsie approached these warily and pushed her nose in amongst the roots. Yes, there it was again! Groping further, Elsie came upon some little hardened pellets that were unmistakably rodent droppings. Not hamster, though, she thought, sniffing thoroughly. Possibly vole. Still, it was the most encouraging sign she had come across so far.

Elsie was so excited by this discovery that she failed to hear the whirring of wings directly above. The wings flapped as the bird descended, and a twig cracked, finally attracting Elsie's attention. She spun round and found herself practically touching its beak.

It was a magpie, its splendid blue-black wings still ruffled slightly from flight. It turned its head, fixing Elsie with a beady eye. It had landed in the clearing, and Elsie was still in the thicket of nettles.

For a full second that seemed to stretch into an hour, Elsie was paralysed. Then her instincts took over and all her muscles contracted at once so that she could dart backwards. But at exactly the same moment, the bird's neck shot forward, the beak plunging into the tangled leaves.

'I said, back off,' snarled the big rat, when the others failed to move. 'This one's mine, I tell you. Clear orf!'

'We found her too,' said one rat, and several others muttered, 'It's not fair!'

The big rat reared even further into the air.

'I got here first,' he said. 'Anyone who wants to object can come and fight it out now, one at a time, single combat.'

No one moved.

'I could take on the whole lot of yer – one arm tied behind me back,' said the big rat. 'Remember what happened the last time there was a dispute – eh? Remember Clint?' He left little Elsie and took one or two steps towards the rat who had objected. 'What happened to Clint?' he asked in a low voice that was almost a whisper. The other rat cowered.

'You – you ate him,' he muttered.

'Louder.'

'You ate him,' the other rat squeaked.

''S'right,' said the biggest rat. 'And very tough he was too. But once I'm peckish I'll try anything. And I must say,' he said, looking round with glinting eyes, 'I'm feeling very peckish at the moment. Starving, in fact.'

All the other rats fell back.

'So if you knows what's good for you,' the biggest rat went on, 'you'll leave, sharpish. NOW!'

All the other rats scarpered.

'Now then, my pretty,' said the biggest rat, turning to little Elsie once more. 'What shall I do with you?' and he grinned unpleasantly. Little Elsie stared back at him.

'You'll leave me alone if you know what's good for you,' she said.

The biggest rat's grin broadened until even the tops

of his yellow teeth were showing, and he pushed her chin up again so far it hurt. 'Will I now?' he said softly, 'and why would I do that?'

Little Elsie twisted away from him. 'I'm not here on my own,' she squeaked. 'You hurt me and they'll come running.'

The biggest rat jerked her head up again, but his eyes were sharp and wary.

'Who will?' he demanded. 'Who'll come running?'

'I will, for one,' said a clear voice directly behind the rat, who spun round, releasing little Elsie so that she staggered and nearly fell. Behind him stood a strange blackish-grey hamster. He seemed young and incredibly dirty. There were so many smudges on his pelt that little Elsie couldn't tell what his true colour might be, and he was nowhere near as big as the rat, but he stood in a warlike pose and seemed more than ready to fight.

'*You!*' snarled the biggest rat. 'You stay out of it! This one's mine!'

The young hamster didn't seem at all daunted. 'I'm sure Rolf'll be interested to hear that,' he said. The biggest rat looked suddenly shifty.

'Rolf?' he said. 'Well – he's not here, is he. So it's none of his business either.' And suddenly his paw shot out and he grabbed little Elsie by the pelt. Little Elsie squeaked aloud as he started to run, dragging her into one of the minor tunnels.

'Drop her, Tyler!' shouted the strange hamster, and he ran after the rat. Little Elsie kicked and dug her heels in and generally tried to make herself as heavy as possible, and Tyler had only taken a few steps when his way was suddenly blocked.

'That's far enough!' said a deep voice, and Tyler stopped so abruptly that he almost fell over. Little Elsie squirmed out of his way just in time. Peering round she saw the biggest, shaggiest rat she had ever seen. She had thought that Tyler was big, but this one was enormous. He seemed to fill the whole tunnel, and he cuffed Tyler so hard that he fell over properly this time. Little Elsie darted backwards and began to run. She ran directly into the strange hamster, squeaking and biting as he held her.

'Steady on!' he exclaimed. '*OW!*'

He released her and she began to calm down, though she still backed away into the main tunnel. 'I – I'm sorry,' she said, unnerved.

There was a terrible squeaking and squealing as the enormous rat laid into Tyler. Little Elsie covered her ears, and the strange hamster guided her away.

'You'll be all right now,' he shouted above the noise. 'My name's Drew, by the way.'

The next moment there was the sound of scuttling paws approaching from one of the other pipes, and Capper, Donal and Tucker burst into the main tunnel.

'What is it – what's going on?' Donal shouted, then, 'Little Elsie – what are you doing here?'

Little Elsie flew towards him. Capper stared in astonishment at the strange hamster.

'Who are you?' he demanded, and Tucker said, 'What's going on?'

Donal looked ready to fight Drew, but little Elsie said hastily, 'It's all right – he saved me.'

Then the squeaking and squealing died away as the enormous rat released Tyler who limped off licking his wounds. And Capper gasped as the biggest rat he had ever seen appeared at the entrance of the tunnel. 'Cripes,' he said nervously, but Tucker said, 'Rolf!' and the big rat said, 'Tucker! What are you doing here?'

Then everyone gathered round, talking at once. It seemed that before Tucker had made his way to The Wild, he had lived in the sewers and had got to know Rolf quite well. It was the same Rolf who, so long ago, had saved Frank from a gang of rats when he had been leading Felicity, Drew, Chestnut and Maurice back to the pet shop. And it had been Tyler who had attacked them then.

'Some rats never learn,' said Rolf. Ever since that time, he had lived in the sewers with Felicity, whom he had loved since the pet shop days, and her cub Drew, who had grown into a fine strong hamster with Rolf as his father: fearless, and a keen hunter. But they were both astonished to hear about the set-up in The Wild.

'You mean – rats and hamsters are living together all the time now?' he kept saying, and Capper said, 'And field mice!'

'And voles and shrews,' put in Donal.

'When I think of the fuss that was made,' Rolf said, 'when me and Felicity wanted to get together.'

'Well, not any more, mate,' said Capper. 'You'd be welcome to live with us.'

'It's for every rodent who needs refuge,' put in little Elsie.

'Except now,' said Tucker solemnly, 'it's all in danger.'

And they explained to Rolf the reason why they had been exploring the sewers, to see if it was safe for everyone in The Wild to shelter there.

'Don't you worry about that,' said Rolf. 'This here's my territory – you can all come, as many as you like.'

Capper, Tucker, Donal and little Elsie all looked at one another with shining eyes.

'It's very decent of you, mate,' Tucker said gruffly, and Rolf said not at all, and Donal and little Elsie jumped up and down crying, 'Let's go and tell Dad!'

'And I'll tell Mum,' said Drew, and he looked at little Elsie. 'You will come back, won't you?' he asked.

Little Elsie blushed. 'Of course I will,' she said, adding hastily, 'and everyone else will too!'

'But first,' Capper said severely, 'we've got to get you back home. Your mum'll be worried sick.'

And there were thanks all round, and promises to meet again, and it was a much happier troop of rodents that set out once more for The Wild, convinced that they had at least a temporary solution to their problems.

Elsie cried aloud as the magpie's beak gashed her. She tried to dart backwards, but was caught in a tangle of bracken. The beak withdrew, then plunged forward again, catching her shoulder. Then suddenly there was a clamour of voices.

'Oi, here – over here!'

'Hey, you! Big Bird! Wotcha doin'?'

It was Boris and Rodney, pelting the magpie with

small stones. Distracted, the bird rose, flapping and squawking into the air.

Boris dashed forward. 'Quick – run!' he shouted.

Elsie didn't need telling twice. She tore herself out of the bracken and followed as fast as she could, with Rodney scampering behind. Fortunately they were only inches away from a burrow. Boris plunged into the entry, followed by Elsie, and Rodney leapt in behind them, yelping as the bird descended again.

They ran through the earthy burrow for several moments, then Boris stopped and turned round. 'Are you all right?' he said. 'It's Elsie, isn't it?'

'Yes,' gasped Elsie. 'I – I think I'm all right.'

She was bleeding a little across the chest and shoulder. Boris examined the wound, shaking his head. 'Lucky we found you,' he said. 'Still – you're safe now.'

Elsie looked at them both. 'How can I ever thank you?' she said.

''S'all right,' said Rodney stoutly. 'If we didn't all fight together, we'd never survive.'

'But what are you doing out here?' Boris wanted to know, and Elsie told them that she had a message for George.

'That's just where we're going!' Rodney said, and Boris shouted, 'Follow me!'

Somewhat shaken by her recent experiences and the loss of blood, Elsie followed. Already the warm burrow seemed more inviting than on previous occasions, because at least now she knew she was safe. She didn't even mind when tiny spiders scuttled across her pelt, and soon she picked up the concentrated scent of rodents, which meant that they were approaching the Great Chamber. A shrew came out to meet them.

'Who is it?' he wanted to know. 'Oh – it's you. You don't happen to have little Elsie with you, do you?'

'No – big Elsie,' said Boris. 'And she's got a message for George. Go and fetch him, will you?'

The little shrew ran off, and Elsie followed Boris into the Great Chamber, feeling once again overwhelmed by the range of different scents filling her nostrils – the scents of voles and field mice and shrews and even rabbits, mingled with the scents of beetles and worms, and a definite, musty smell of disturbed earth. If she had been alone, the strangeness of it might have overwhelmed her, but as it was, she recovered quickly and looked round eagerly for George.

Soon George appeared, looking very worried and harrassed. 'Elsie?' he called. Elsie ran up to him and fell into his arms.

'Oh, Elsie,' he murmured, hugging her. 'I've been so worried –' Then he broke off, holding her at arm's length. 'You're bleeding!' he exclaimed.

'Oh, don't worry, George – it's only a scratch,' said Elsie. 'I'm fine now I'm here – with you. But where's Daisy?'

Daisy was in a burrow of her own, having her babies. 'And little Elsie's gone missing, and I daren't tell her,' said George, looking more worried than ever, 'and half this Chamber's fallen in – and – Elsie – I don't know what to do!'

Elsie hugged him again. 'Don't worry, George, dear,' she said, 'I've come to help –' and she was about to tell him her idea when suddenly, there was a commotion and two shrews came bursting in.

'We've found little Elsie!' they cried. 'We've found her – we've found her!'

'I wasn't lost,' said little Elsie with dignity, walking in ahead of Donal, Capper and Tucker.

George bounded towards her. 'Oh, where've you been?' he cried, shaking and hugging her at once.

'She was following us,' said Capper.

'You naughty girl!' cried George, kissing her several times.

Little Elsie pulled away. 'Don't you want to hear our news?' she said.

George wiped a tear from his eye. 'I just wanted you back,' he said. 'We've all been worried sick. I didn't dare tell your mother!'

Little Elsie had the grace to look a bit ashamed. 'Sorry, Dad,' she said, 'but really we've got wonderful news. We've saved the colony!'

George looked from little Elsie to Donal, Capper and Tucker. 'What do you mean?' he demanded. 'What's happened?'

All four of them tried to explain at once about meeting Rolf and Drew in the sewers, and how Rolf had said that there was plenty of room for everyone, and they would be perfectly safe. Elsie remembered Felicity and Drew very well and she clasped her paws in amazement as little Elsie told them how Drew had saved her from the rat.

George looked at Capper in astonishment, then back to Donal and little Elsie. 'So . . . this means . . .' he said slowly.

'That we can all go there – right away!' cried little Elsie. 'Shall I go and tell everyone now?'

'Wait a minute – just hold on,' said George, getting flustered. 'Did anyone explore the other sites? What about the substation?' he said, looking at Boris and Rodney, but Boris shook his head. 'No go, Boss,' he said. 'Looks like work's started in that area.'

'If we're going to move, we should move quickly,' Capper urged, 'and make sure everyone gets out of the burrows.'

Everyone looked at George, but George didn't speak. The thought of leaving The Wild was a huge one for him, and he had hated the sewers – nasty, dank, evil-smelling places, flooded at regular intervals by filthy water. And there were all the hostile rats. Was it any place to take the new cubs, he wondered. He looked at Elsie.

'What do you think?' he said.

Elsie unclasped her paws, then clasped them again. She took a deep breath.

'Well,' she said, 'there is another way – if we're brave enough.' And she told them what Lucy had told her, that if a rare or endangered species was found in The Wild, the building would have to stop.

There was complete silence for a few moments after she finished speaking, then George said slowly, 'But that would mean –'

'Letting ourselves be caught,' Boris finished for him, and he snorted. 'No way!' There was a babble of voices.

'We'd be taken captive again!'

'We'd lose the colony straight off!'

'We might as well stay here and wait for the builders to destroy it!'

Elsie looked unhappily from one speaker to another. Most of these rodents had had terrible experiences with humans, whereas her own experience with Lucy had been good. She was hardly in a position to tell them that they had to give people one last chance. And really, even to her, it seemed like a terrible risk.

George was still looking at her and picking up on her thoughts as he often did. He couldn't help shuddering. 'You really think it's a risk we should take?' he said in a low voice, and Elsie knew he was remembering Jake and Josh.

'No, Dad, no!' said Declan and Donal. They too had heard the horror stories of Jake and Josh, and of what had happened to their mother when she'd been kept in a hamster circus.

Elsie felt more miserable than ever. It seemed that she alone stood on the side of the humans, and this made her feel lonely and cut off from her kind. She wondered, briefly, what Frank would say. She couldn't imagine that he would be on the humans' side either. She cleared her throat.

'I only think,' she began, 'that to move the whole colony into the sewers is also difficult and dangerous – and it's only a temporary solution. What happens if there *is* no Wild when you come back? Whereas, if my plan works, it might be a permanent solution – it might mean that The Wild is preserved.'

There was some muttering at this. 'It's a big "if",' Boris said, and little Elsie, thinking of Drew, said, 'I want to go back!' George looked bewildered. 'Capper?' he said, but Capper shook his head. 'It's up to you,' he said.

There was a silence, which might have gone on a long time, but suddenly a female hamster came hurrying along a burrow at the far end of the Great Chamber.

'The cubs have arrived!' she announced, beaming. 'Another six fine healthy babies!'

There was a half-hearted cheer at this, and some further muttering. George's face lit up. Hope and fear flitted across it.

'Oh, can we see them? Can we see them?' cried little Elsie, Donal and Declan, and Elsie pressed George's paw. 'Yes, George, you must,' she said firmly. 'The decision can wait.' And paw in paw they advanced towards the burrow, with little Elsie, Donal and Declan scampering ahead.

At the entrance to the burrow, George paused as though to say something to Elsie. His face was full of anxiety and love. He opened his mouth to speak and she squeezed his paw encouragingly.

But the next moment, the whole of the Great Chamber was violently rocked. The rodents were flung backwards, as, with a grinding and tearing noise, a huge metal claw descended, penetrating the earth. Elsie glimpsed the dull orange metal in front of her before she rolled over and over and lay stunned. The burrow ahead of them was ripped away. Amid the cries and shrieks and lamentations, she heard one voice raised above all the others.

'Daisy!' George cried in anguish, and he clawed his way desperately over the rubble towards the place where the burrow had been. 'Daisy! No! Oh, no, Daisy – no!'

10 Alone

'No?' Frank said, unable to believe it. '*No?*'

Shocked to the core, he could feel the dark place in the depths of his mind disappearing as though wrenched away, and though he resisted with all his might, he was returning to ordinary consciousness. The lab and the perspex unit in which he was enclosed were returning with horrible clarity. He kept his eyes closed and leaned against the wall of the unit, breathing hard.

His first thought was that he must have got it wrong. The Black Hamster had helped him time and time again – he never said 'No'! Frank would simply have to try again.

And he did try, several times, but it was as though an invisible barrier had rolled down between him and the point of contact with the Black Hamster.

It was as though the Black Hamster had simply shut the door.

When he finally realized this, Frank opened his eyes. He stared around for a moment, as if he couldn't quite believe his surroundings, as if they made no sense. Then he gave a short, nervous laugh and licked his lips. It was a joke, it had to be. Any moment now the Black

Hamster would be there in the laboratory with Frank. Frank would see the ruby glow of his eyes and feel the velvety softness of his magnificent pelt. He ran from one side of the perspex unit to the other, pressing his paws against the panes.

If it was a joke, it wasn't funny. Frank couldn't see, hear or even smell the Black Hamster anywhere, and even the voice that had spoken to him earlier seemed to have disappeared. No one was there apart from Frank and Leila, who was still apparently unconscious It was no use to carry on searching and hoping; Frank was wasting his time.

Once he had realized this, Frank stood absolutely still in the centre of the perspex unit. As hope left him, he drooped further and further towards the floor. It was as if all his energy was draining away.

Then slowly, the thought he had been fending off came to him and seemed to eat away at his heart. The words Mabel had said to him, so long ago, slid irresistibly into his mind.

The Black Hamster is a force that Lures, she had said. *In the dead of night he comes, to Lure them to the Dark Places and beyond, even to the Pits of Doom.*

Frank had never been quite able to imagine what a Pit of Doom might look like. He had certainly never envisaged a laboratory. But if this place with its unnatural smells of chemicals and despair wasn't a Pit of Doom, then what was it? This was it, he told himself, and he slumped even further so that he was crouching down. He had been Lured. Worse than that, he had been betrayed.

Now Frank knew the bitterness of real despair. Yet even in the midst of it, the tiny part of his brain that was still functioning addressed him sternly in a practical manner.

'Now this isn't any good, is it?' and 'You won't get anywhere moping about on your rear end, you know,' and 'What are you going to do about it, eh?' and 'Think, Frank, think!'

It was like a little monitor, nudging the rest of him into activity, into remembering where he was, and who he was and why he was there. And as it went on nagging him, Frank remembered something else as well – a voice from another part of his mind that spoke faintly, as though very far away.

It said, 'Courage!'

Frank listened, because he couldn't help himself, and it spoke again.

'Courage!' it said.

It was as though the star he had seen in the darkness was still burning, though the darkness had gone.

'Courage!'

Because, before Frank had ever relied on the Black Hamster, he'd had to rely on himself. And he was still here, still alive and breathing. He wasn't even alone. There were all these other hamsters to rescue.

Frank lifted his head again and looked around. The first thing was to get out of this unit. It was obvious what he had to do, but rather less obvious how he was going to do it.

'Think, Frank,' said one voice, and 'Courage!' said the other.

Frank thought. He had already managed to control Vernon once, and he was obviously going to have to do it again. At least, he couldn't see any other way out of the container. But then, once he'd got Vernon to release them all, he had to have a plan. However was he going to get all these hamsters back to Bright Street?

Suddenly, Frank bristled all over as Marcia spoke quite close to him. He hadn't even noticed that she'd come in.

'Well, one of us will have to go to the pet shop,' she said. 'And I want to be here when the supplies arrive. You can take the car.'

Vernon grumbled a bit, but Frank wasn't listening. His mind was racing. Somehow, he had to get Vernon to take all the hamsters back to the pet shop with him. It flashed across his mind that even if Vernon only took Frank, he would still be able to raise the alarm once he got back to Bright Street, and get Guy to investigate or tell the police; but that would mean leaving all the hamsters with Marcia, who might carry out more of her awful experiments once he'd gone. And then there was Leila. Frank didn't ever want to leave Leila again. No: either they all got out or none of them would.

Frank jumped as Marcia's enormous face loomed over his unit. She gazed at him with her cool green eyes, exactly as if she was dissecting him.

'Once the van arrives we can start the steroid drip,' she murmured. Frank glared at her defiantly, putting all his rage and hatred into the glare, and she laughed admiringly. 'What a fighter you'll be,' she said, then she passed on to Leila's unit.

'My poor, pretty girl,' she murmured soothingly as Leila twitched. Then she stood up and spoke to Vernon in quite a different tone. 'I'm afraid this one's done for,' she said. 'Put her in the incinerator with the other rejects, would you?'

Frank's heart leapt in horror and anguish, but Vernon merely said that he'd see to it when he got back, and he carried on cleaning out equipment in the sink. That settled it, Frank thought. No more hamsters were going to suffer that awful fate, least of all Leila. He had to get them all out now.

'I'll be in reception if you need me,' Marcia said. 'I've got a few phone calls to make.'

Frank heard her high heels click, click, clicking over the laboratory floor, then the sound of the door as it opened and shut. This was it! He was on his own with Vernon. Now he had to establish control of his mind.

Sometimes, when you want to do a thing very much, it's almost as if the need to do it gets in the way. Frank's urgency was making it difficult to concentrate. He shut his eyes and tried to see Vernon's face. 'Release the hamsters!' he commanded, but Vernon went on humming tunelessly and splashing about in the sink.

He thought harder, trying to sense his thoughts going over to Vernon. 'Release the hamsters!' he demanded.

Nothing. There was a loud clattering noise as Vernon gathered all his implements together on a tray. Panic and desperation rose in Frank. He was going to fail, just as he'd failed to contact the Black Hamster. But he couldn't fail now, he just couldn't.

All at once it was as though Frank's body remembered how to do it, in spite of him. He put his shoulders back and straightened his spine. He took a deep breath and felt his consciousness moving inwards, backwards and down. Past the jumble of thoughts and images in his mind it went, sinking into the darkness that had escaped him before. And, yes! There it was – the silvery light, like a cord. He had to hold on to it somehow and move it towards Vernon.

The silvery cord wreathed around the room like smoke, from Frank all the way over to Vernon. Frank could feel it reach him and give a little tug.

'Release the hamsters, Vernon,' he said.

Vernon stopped humming at once. 'What – all of them?' he said aloud.

'All of them,' said Frank, 'beginning with me.'

He shuddered a little as Vernon obeyed him, walking all the way over to Frank's unit and releasing the catches at the side that let the front down. Then, resisting this time the impulse to run, he allowed Vernon to pick him up in his fat pink paws and carry him through to the room in which all the other hamsters were held captive. He knew that he had to maintain the contact of the silvery cord all the time.

Several of the hamsters looked up in dull amazement to see Frank being carried in Vernon's hands, but they didn't say anything. Mabel, however, had something to say.

'Frank!' she hissed. 'Where've you been — you've been gone ages — we all thought you'd run off and left us — saved your own skin — I —'

'Shut up, Mabel,' said Frank shortly. He had no time for explanations. He raised his voice.

'Listen, all of you,' he said. 'In a moment this man is going to release you all. He will put you —' Frank glanced quickly round the room, searching for a suitable mode of transport, and his gaze fell on a sort of long tray on wheels, like a hospital trolley '— on to the long tray and take you out to the car. Then he will drive us all to the pet shop. Fill your pouches now and be ready when he opens up your units.'

When Frank finished speaking, there was complete silence. Then one of the glowing rabbits said slowly, 'I don't understand.'

'You don't need to understand,' snapped Frank. 'Just do what I say — *now*!' As he spoke Frank felt a surge of dark energy welling from the pit of his stomach. He had felt it once before when addressing the new colony of hamsters in The Wild, and this time, as before, the hamsters must have felt it too, because they immediately started filling their pouches.

'Take me to the trolley,' Frank commanded Vernon and Vernon did as he was told, lowering Frank on to the steel tray on wheels. Then he began to wheel it round to each of the units in turn, unfastening the catches and lowering the front pane. The hamsters stared in dull amazement, but one by one even the most disabled hobbled on to the trolley. Mabel had stuffed so much food into her pouches that she looked almost circular by the time the trolley reached her, but she too waddled on to the trolley without question. Once on it the hamsters began whispering amongst themselves in a worried kind of way.

'What's going on?'

'What's happening?'

'Where's he taking us?'

Frank ignored them. He knew he had to keep the thread of his concentration unbroken, not even interrupting it to think, 'It's working!' as Vernon wheeled them all towards the door. Besides, he had to work out the best way for them all to leave the building so that Marcia wouldn't see. And they still had to collect Leila.

'Take me to Leila,' Frank said to Vernon in his mind, and at once Vernon changed course and began to wheel them all towards the laboratory. He stopped beside the long bench and Frank leapt off immediately and ran towards Leila, his heart racing.

'Leila!' he gasped as he reached her unit. 'Wake up!'

Leila's eyes opened vaguely. 'Oh, it's you,' she said wonderingly. 'I was dreaming about you.'

Frank didn't waste time asking about the dream. 'I've come to get you out of here,' he said. 'Vernon's going to open the unit and take these tubes out, and we're going – we're all going to escape!'

Leila lifted her head, trying unsuccessfully to see.

'But how −?' she began.

'No time to explain,' said Frank. He ran round the unit trying to see exactly where Leila was attached to all the drips. 'We've got to get all these tube thingies out of you and −'

Leila was shaking her head. 'It won't work,' she sighed and her head drooped on to her paws again.

'Don't say that,' said Frank. 'We've just got to get you out of here, and we'll get you well in no time.'

But Leila shook her head again. 'There's no point,' she said. 'I can't do anything without the tubes. I can't move or breathe. They're keeping me alive.'

Frank stared at her, his lips suddenly dry. 'What do you mean?' he said.

Leila looked at him, but her gaze seemed far away. 'I mean that without the tubes, I die,' she said.

This was the worst news Frank had ever had. He gazed at his mother, unable to think what to do. From the trolley there rose an impatient murmur.

'What's he doing?'

'Are we leaving, or what?'

And from reception he could hear Marcia talking on the phone. 'It's a pleasure doing business with you,' she said. 'We'll be in touch. Bye for now.'

'I'm not leaving you here!' he said desperately. 'We − we'll take you in the unit!'

Leila sighed, a little breath full of frailty and despair. 'There's no point,' she said. 'Just go.'

'I can't!' said Frank. As he looked at her, he thought that now might be the time to tell her everything. He pressed his paws against the pane of the unit.

'Leila,' he said. 'Leila, do you know who I am?'

Leila looked at him, but the beautiful eyes were blank. Frank licked his lips. 'My name's Frank,' he said, and just for a moment he thought he could see the echo of a memory stirring in Leila's eyes.

'Frank,' she said faintly.

Frank held his breath, willing her to remember him, but from reception, Marcia's voice interrupted them again.

'The deal's on,' she said. 'Vernon, isn't it time you were going?'

Frank willed Vernon to say nothing and Vernon didn't speak. But the flicker of recognition had gone from Leila's eyes.

'Time's running out,' Frank said. 'We'll take you in your unit.'

'No!' said Leila, in a stronger voice than Frank had heard from her before. She tried to raise herself, but sank back feebly. 'We need to disconnect the tubes,' she said.

'But you said —' Frank began.

'I know what I said,' Leila told him, and she turned her beautiful face towards Frank.

'My time is over,' she said. 'I want to feel again what it's like to breathe naturally, and for my heart to beat on its own —'

'No!' cried Frank. He pressed his paws to the perspex. 'I can't let you die — I won't! You're coming with me!'

'Listen to me, Frank,' said Leila, and there was a new tone of authority in her voice. 'I've had enough. I don't want to live like this. I want to die.'

Frank stared at her and he knew it was true. He felt as though his world was crumbling around him. 'But Leila,' he whispered, and Leila held her paw towards his.

'Do it for me, Frank,' she said.

Frank pulled his paws away. It was horrible, horrible. He dashed a tear from his eye. 'I can't stand by and let that man kill you!' he cried. 'I can't let him take the tubes out! I can't and I won't!'

Leila's eyes flickered. 'Then you do it, Frank,' she said.

Frank stared at her once more. Behind him all the hamsters were getting nervous and twitchy. 'What's happening?' said one, and 'Why aren't we moving?' said another, and 'She's coming, she's coming!' said a third. Suddenly, Mabel's voice rose above the others.

'Oi, Frank! What's going on?' she said loudly. 'Get a move on!'

'Leila,' said Frank, 'I can't.'

Leila's eyes closed.

'Come *on*,' said several of the hamsters, and 'Leave her there if she doesn't want to come,' and 'You're risking our lives!'

'All *right*!' snapped Frank, over his shoulder. Then he turned back to Leila. He saw, with a dreadful clarity, what had to be done. At Frank's command, Vernon opened the cage. But Frank wouldn't let him touch the tubes. He looked at them. They were everywhere: in her heart, stomach, lungs, spine. He put out one paw, touching his mother for the first time since he was a tiny cub. Then very gently, he withdrew the needle at the back of her neck. Leila opened her eyes and smiled.

With one part of his mind, Frank knew his heart was breaking. This was Leila, his mother, whom he would never know and who would never know him. But he couldn't allow that part to think. He couldn't bear to dwell on the details of her suffering, or on the fact that he would never see her again. Another part of his mind was cold as ice, almost frozen, pulling the tubes out smoothly, smoothly, doing the necessary thing. This was the part that was still trying to calculate how to get all the hamsters out without Marcia Taylor noticing. And yet a third part of his mind was acting in deep obedience to his mother, and to the ancient, unwritten law that says every animal knows when the time has come, and has the right to die. He kept his eyes on Leila's face the whole time and he knew it was an image he would never forget. And Leila looked at Frank, and went on looking sightlessly at him, only wincing once or twice when a needle tugged.

It was the worst, the hardest thing he had ever done. And all the time he was thinking that now Leila would never know he was her son. He hesitated a long moment before pulling out the needle from her heart, and as he did it he felt the bitterness of absolute despair. Leila gave a little sigh and closed her eyes.

'That's it, then,' Frank thought, and he leaned forward to say the word 'Mother,' but he couldn't speak.

But Leila's eyelids fluttered and she opened them one last time. Impossibly, she raised a fragile, trembling paw towards Frank's face. Her lips moved, and Frank hunched over her, desperately trying to hear.

'I know you,' she whispered. 'You are my own sweet cub.' Then the beautiful eyes clouded over and something that was in Leila left, very peacefully. Her paw dropped back on to her chest.

All the hamsters behind Frank were silent, despite their fears, for every animal acknowledges the presence of death. Frank felt hot tears dropping on to Leila's pelt. He remained hunched over her, unable to move. He felt as though his eyes had opened on to darkness.

Somewhere, in the depths of his despair, there was anger, and it wasn't anger at the humans who had done this monstrous thing, or at the injustice that all animals suffer, though both these were elements of his rage. But at the heart of it, there was a small, burning core that prevented him from lapsing wholly into overwhelming grief; and this part, this white-hot spark, was directed against the being he had come to love and trust above all others, who had led him here and betrayed him.

'Why, why?' this part of him raged. 'Why have you deserted me?' and he looked wildly up and around, as though hoping even now that the Black Hamster would appear. But nothing happened, and Frank lifted his voice and uttered the long, terrible call of grief that made all the listening hamsters shiver on their trolley.

'Vernon?' came Marcia's piercing voice. 'Vernon? What are you *doing* in there?' And all the hamsters clutched one another in fear as they heard the sound of a chair being pushed back and sharp heels clicking across the floor.

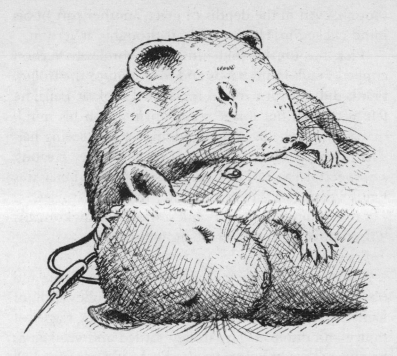

Vernon's head jerked and he made a funny little rasping noise. He lifted one hand to his forehead and rubbed it as though trying to stimulate his brain to think.

'I . . . don't . . . know,' he said wonderingly.

'Frank!' hissed Mabel in fear. 'Frank – do something!'

Frank remained hunched over the body of Leila and all the hamsters began twittering in fear. The door to the laboratory opened . . . and the phone rang. Marcia made a little 'Tsk-tsk' noise and tapped back across the room to answer it. Slowly, Frank's shoulders straightened and he took a long, shaky breath. It was as though, even in the depths of grief, another part of his mind clicked in. He directed his thoughts at Vernon.

'Pick me up,' he told him, and wordlessly Vernon cupped Frank in his hands and took him to the trolley. Frank did not turn round for a final look at Leila; he felt as though her image was imprinted on his mind, that as long as he lived he would never stop seeing her. The other hamsters moved over on the trolley, creating a respectful space. They didn't know that Leila was Frank's dam, but they could sense his terrible grief.

Little Lugs touched Frank's shoulder awkwardly. 'Glad you're with us, Frank,' he whispered.

Frank said nothing.

'Take us out the back way,' he instructed Vernon, and obediently Vernon set off with the trolley full of hamsters, maybe thirty or more, in various stages of injury and disrepair. The trolley rattled and clanked as he approached the door at the back of the lab and all the hamsters clung to one another and to the rail to stop themselves falling off. Except for Frank, who stood quite alone in the middle.

'Open the door,' he said to Vernon, and Vernon did as he was told, although he had some trouble tugging the trolley through it and down the little step.

'Right then – bye,' Marcia said on the phone, and the next moment all the hamsters heard her footsteps once more. 'Now then, Vernon, what *are* you doing? Haven't you set off yet?'

'Say something,' Frank told Vernon, and Vernon said, 'We're just setting off now.'

'*We?*' said Marcia suspiciously, and she opened the

door. At the same moment, Vernon jerked the trolley, tugging it through and the door slammed shut behind them. They were off, rolling through the freezing air towards the vivid green sports car that would take them away from the dreadful laboratory forever.

11 Rescue

George scrabbled away at the rubble like a mad hamster.

'Daisy – Daisy!' he sobbed.

Slowly, Elsie picked herself up. All around her, shrews and hamsters and voles lay moaning in the overturned earth. She pulled her hind paws free and hobbled over to George. She put a paw on his shoulder and spoke to him, but he didn't hear.

'Daisy – the cubs!' he wept.

All the burrows in front of them had collapsed. It looked very much as though Daisy and the cubs and the babies would be buried under all the earth, but Elsie couldn't let herself think about that. She clutched George's shoulder, but he shook her off.

'Daisy,' he moaned.

'George,' Elsie said, 'George, dear, we've got to get out.'

George ignored her. He ran to another mound of rubble and began tunnelling furiously, uselessly.

Behind Elsie, Boris appeared. 'We'd best get to the sewers,' he said, 'before it happens again.'

George turned round at this. His eyes were wild.

'I'm not leaving them!' he cried.

'George, listen to me,' said Elsie in a shaky voice. 'We can't stay here. The big machines have started, George; if we stay here we'll all be lost.'

'I don't care!' George cried shrilly, and he turned back to the rubble, tearing at it with his paws. Capper, Rodney and a few others gathered round.

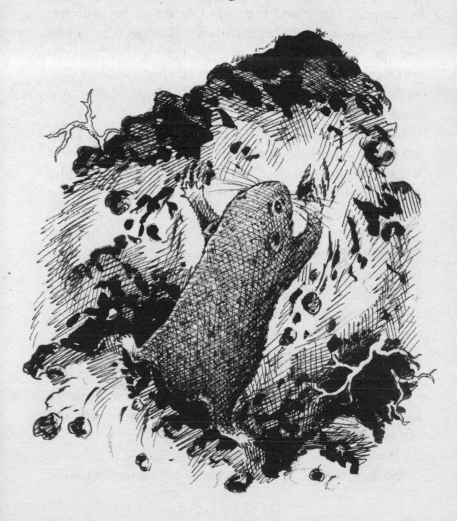

'Come on, Boss,' Boris began.

'NO!' George shrieked.

Elsie, Boris and Capper exchanged worried looks. 'If we get out now,' Capper murmured, 'we stand a chance. If not . . .'

He didn't finish the sentence, but Elsie knew what he was trying to say. But George wouldn't leave while he thought Daisy and the cubs might still be in there, and Elsie wasn't prepared to leave George. She licked her lips.

'George,' she began, then more sternly, 'George!' She went over to him and shook him. 'George – stop it at once!'

George turned to Elsie and clutched her pelt. 'Help me find them, Elsie!' he begged.

Elsie could see that his heart was breaking. She could see it and feel it in her own heart. She blinked and swallowed.

'George – you can't help them like this . . .' she said, but suddenly she didn't know how to go on. 'I wish Frank was here!' she burst out miserably. George pulled away from her. His eyes were wild once more.

'Frank?' he cried. 'Where is he? Not here – Oh, no – not in this place – he wouldn't come here –'

Elsie looked at him as though she thought he was raving. 'What do you mean?' she said.

George's voice rose shrilly and spittle flew from his lips. 'Not good enough – not good enough for Frank!' He laughed. 'I saw the look in his eyes!'

'What are you talking about?' cried Elsie.

'Not *his* place – not Frank's own place!' George

ranted on. 'He didn't want to live here – he was going to warn us, he said, warn us of any danger – So tell me this, Elsie – *why didn't he warn us about the big machines?*'

Elsie was speechless for a moment as the implications of what George was saying sank in. 'What?' she whispered. 'What are you saying?'

There was a mad, triumphant look in George's eyes. 'Because he didn't want it to work, that's why – he never wanted the New Narkiz to survive!'

There was a shocked silence from everyone in the ruined chamber, then, without thinking, Elsie stepped forward and cuffed George hard.

'Don't you ever talk about Frank like that again,' she said in low, terrible tones, surprising even herself. 'He would never betray us – he's our friend! He's risked his life for us time and time again! He . . .'

Elsie's words ran out and she could only glower at George, who stared back at her with a mixture of astonished pain and defiance in his eyes. Then suddenly he sagged backwards against a pile of rubble and wept openly.

'I'm sorry,' he cried, clasping the sides of his head with his paws. 'I don't know what to do – I'm sorry – I'm sorry, sorry!'

Many of the other hamsters, shrews and voles wept with him, but as Elsie looked at him she felt suddenly clear and calm.

'We can't stay here,' she said sternly. 'We can't help Daisy and the cubs unless we save ourselves. We've got to get out – any way we can. Once we're clear, we'll go back to the surface and search for them, George – do you understand?' She shook him by the shoulder and he nodded miserably. Then she turned to Boris, Rodney and Capper.

'Can you get us out of here?' she said.

'We'll try,' said Capper, and Boris said, 'We'll give it our best shot.'

Elsie tugged George to his feet. 'Then lead the way!' she said.

Vernon shot through another red light in the green sports car.

'Woooo!' cried the hamsters as they were flattened backwards by the speed, and 'Whoa!' as he swung round a corner and they all lurched to one side.

'What's happening?' cried one, and 'Make it stop!' whimpered another.

Mabel struggled to free herself from a heap of squirming hamsters. 'What's going on?' she shouted, glaring at Frank. 'Stop it at once!' Then she disappeared again as Vernon hurtled round another bend.

Frank thought he knew what was going on. He had taken control of the part of Vernon's mind that was responsible for driving. And of course, Frank knew next to nothing about the Highway Code, and he couldn't drive at all. So Vernon was shooting through traffic and had already nearly mown down two pedestrians. It was highly dangerous, but Frank hardly cared. Mabel, however, cared very much. She elbowed her way to the top of the pile and clambered over the other hamsters, cuffing them out of the way.

'Do something!' she demanded. 'Are you trying to get us all killed?'

Frank looked at Mabel. 'We're nearly there,' he said, then he was buffeted to one side as Mellor landed on him.

'I don't care!' Mabel howled. 'Whatever it is you're doing – stop it now!'

The problem was that if Frank released control of Vernon's mind, he wouldn't take them all to Bright Street as Frank hoped. He would drive them to the pet shop, as Marcia had told him to, and then they'd be on their own. Worst of all, he might drive them all back to the laboratory. Frank glared at Mabel and didn't answer, but suddenly, there was a screech of brakes and several horns sounded at once, almost deafening the hamsters. Vernon hardly faltered, but swerved round the pile-up of traffic, throwing all the hamsters to one side again.

'We might as well have died in the laboratory!' honked the hamster with the elephant trunk.

Frank sighed. He could see that Vernon might cause a major accident. Or that, at the rate they were going, they might never reach the pet shop. Reluctantly, he let go of Vernon's mind, and at once the car slowed down.

'About time!' snapped Mabel. 'Some of us want to get home in one piece!'

'We might not get home at all now!' retorted Frank. 'So I hope you've got some ideas!'

The rest of the journey passed without incident, and soon the car was slowing down outside the pet shop. Frank thought quickly. He had to regain his hold over

Vernon long enough for him to let them out; then they would all have to cross the pavement without anyone seeing them and hide. And from then on, he didn't know what they would do.

On Frank's command, Vernon opened the car door and left it open. One by one the hamsters dropped into the muddy space between the car and the kerb. They huddled together, watching all the different kinds of human feet pass by on the pavement: big boots, trainers, platform heels.

At last, when there was a gap in the people walking by, Frank whispered, 'Now!' and they scrambled up the kerb and ran across the pavement as fast as they could, hearts thudding, whiskers whipping the air, towards a little alley at the side of the pet shop where a number of wheelie bins were kept. Last of all came Frank, shepherding the slowest and those hampered by injury to safety. The fear of discovery pricked the back of his neck, but most humans don't really notice what's going on around their feet and two elderly ladies passed by, deep in conversation, without noticing a thing. At last, all the hamsters were safely huddled into the space between the wheelie bins and the pet-shop wall.

'Now what?' said Mabel.

Frank was worried. But the sense of danger had cleared his head, even of grief, and he was thinking hard. They could wait until Vernon had gone and then all troop into the pet shop, but the trouble was that he didn't know what Mr Wiggs would do. He might keep them there until he could sell them all off again – and that was the last thing Frank wanted. He wanted to take them all to George in The Wild.

'Well?' said Mabel. 'Hurry up – I'm freezing!'

Frank ignored her.

Another option was to try to sneak back into the pet shop and make their way into the sewers, and attempt to find their way back to Bright Street from there. Of course the water would be freezing at this time of year, and Frank wasn't entirely sure he knew the way. And they would have to tackle the rats, if they found them. But the only other way was to go through the streets, with all the traffic . . .

'Get a move on!' Mabel said. 'First you try to get us all killed in the car; now you're freezing us to death!'

'I'll tell you what, Mabel,' Frank snapped. 'Why don't you come up with a plan? Hm? You're good at telling everyone else what to do – so go on then – tell us!'

He fixed Mabel with his hardest stare and Mabel shrank back, muttering that she thought he was the one with the ideas.

'Shut up, Mabel,' said Lugs and one or two of the others joined in. 'Yes, shut up,' they said and waited, shivering, for Frank to tell them what to do.

All at once Frank had the glimmerings of an idea. He wasn't sure that he could pull it off because it involved contacting Guy, and he had never been able to contact Guy, or anyone else, when they weren't actually in the same room as him, but he had to try. He took a step or two away from the other hamsters and closed his eyes. He tried to feel himself sinking into the darkness to the point where he could sense the silvery light.

'Guy,' he murmured, then louder and more commandingly, 'Guy!'

Meanwhile, Jake, Josh and Thomas had come home from school and were playing a game of cricket on The Wild, while to one side of them, the big machinery roared and plunged its way into the earth. They weren't really supposed to play near the big machines, but Thomas's mum had taken Lucy to the dentist and Jackie should have been keeping an eye on them, but she was on the phone.

'Fore!' yelled Thomas as he batted the ball high into the air; then all three boys watched in dismay as it landed on the other side of the cordoned-off area.

'Now look what you've done,' said Jake.

'I'm going to get it,' said Thomas.

'You're not allowed!' said Jake, trying to pull him back, but Thomas tore free, and before anyone could stop him, he had ducked under the orange ribbon that marked the building site. He glanced quickly at the men in hard hats, but they were discussing something important about drainage and they all had their backs to him, so he scouted round for his ball, which seemed to have landed in a soft pile of overturned earth.

Thomas scrambled quickly up the pile. He was one of the best in his class at climbing and could shin up ropes and walls with footholds faster than anyone, but this time he wasn't quite fast enough. One of the hard hats turned round.

'Hoy!' he cried.

Thomas lunged for the ball. But just as his fingers

closed round it, he saw something that stopped him in his tracks, even while the overseer and all the men were hurrying towards him. For there, in a little indentation in the pile of earth, was a mother hamster, surrounded by a number of cubs. Thomas stared, then he came to his senses as the overseer caught hold of his coat, and he slithered down the pile.

'Caught you!' said the overseer. 'Now, just what do you think you're playing at?'

But Thomas was waving his arms furiously at his friends. 'Jake, Josh!' he yelled. 'Get your mum – quick!'

★

Guy stood in the middle of the road with his lollipop sign, guiding the older children across. The secondary school children came out later than the ones at the junior school, but Guy stayed out and made sure that they all crossed the busy main road safely. He was on friendly terms with quite a few of the children, and ignored the ones who gave him cheek, but today he was too busy with his own thoughts to stop and chat. He was worried about Frank, who had got out of his cage again. Of course, he had done this many times before, but Guy never stopped worrying about it. And he was worried about the building on The Wild, and how he and Jackie weren't having any success trying to stop it. He was also thinking about asking Jackie out on a proper date, once they had got the protest about the new housing development out of the way. He might even ask her if she wanted to come and see his band – that's if they ever got another gig. They hadn't gone down too well at the Old People's Home and he wasn't sure that they would be asked back. So one way or another, he had a lot to think about, and this stopped him chatting to the parents as he usually did, or even responding to the children when they called out.

'Thanks, Guy!'

'See you tomorrow!'

One of the girls moved her finger round and round at the side of her head as she passed to indicate that he was more than usually away with the fairies. And he was in this dreamy, absent-minded state when he heard the call.

'Guy!' Faintly at first, and far away, then clearer,

'Guy!' And finally, more insistent and demanding. 'GUY!'

And without a word, Guy picked up his lollipop, and leaving the astonished children, walked along the main road towards the pet shop.

'I don't care what your orders are,' Jackie said. 'You've got to stop this work now!'

The overseer squared his shoulders and pushed his hard hat further back on his head. 'Look at it this way, love,' he said. 'You've got a job to do – and I've got a job to do. You – me – we've both got jobs.' He waved an arm expansively. 'All these people around here – they've all got jobs to do. That's what makes the world go round,' he said.

But Jackie wasn't going to be put off. 'You've just dug up a mother hamster and her baby cubs,' she said. 'For all you know, there could be more of them down there. I'm sure the Countryside Agency'll be interested in hamsters in The Wild. And don't call me love,' she added.

'Well, I don't care if I've dug up the Loch Ness Monster and the Missing Link,' said the overseer. 'I've got my schedule. So if you'll just step aside –'

'I'm not going anywhere!' said Jackie. 'Jake, Josh – fetch a box for the hamsters, will you?'

As Jake and Josh and Thomas ran off, Jackie took out her mobile phone. 'Now,' she said. 'Let's see what the press have to say about this, shall we? The *Chronicle*, the *Reporter*, that nice man on local radio –'

'All right, all right,' said the overseer, holding up his

hands. 'You win. Break it up, lads,' he called to the men operating the machinery. 'Take a break. Smell the roses.'

And as the machinery ground and juddered to a halt, and Jackie phoned the press and the Countryside Agency, Jake, Josh and Thomas ran back to the building site carrying a cardboard box lined with newspaper. They scrambled up the heap of loose earth to the top, where a terrified Daisy still lay suckling her newborn cubs, while the older cubs stood protectively around. They had a bit of a job getting them all into the cardboard box, because Donal, Declan, Danny, Dermot, Dean and little Elsie all defended Daisy fiercely, but Jake and Josh had gloves in their pockets, and eventually they managed to lower them in safely.

And so it was that, for the second time in hamster history, a mother and her twelve cubs were found by humans, and carried into human territory, away from their own environment in The Wild.

12 The Last Journey

Meanwhile, Elsie, George and the rest of the colony made their way slowly through crumbling earth towards the sewers. George felt as though he was in a dark dream. His mind was numb; he was just doing as he was told. Boris, Rodney and Tucker, together with two moles, were doing most of the work, clearing the way at the front of the group. George hung further and further behind. At first, Elsie had hung on to him, making sure he kept up, but there had been several minor falls of earth and she'd had to help some of the smallest shrews out. Slowly they were becoming separated. From time to time Elsie would call out, 'George? Are you there?' and George would remember to answer, 'Yes, Elsie, I'm here,' but he felt as though that was only partly true. Only his paws and pelt were there; his heart and mind were lost with Daisy and the cubs and the New Narkiz that he had worked so hard to build.

Gradually, though, his nose began sending him messages. It told him that they were nearing the edge of The Wild, where patchy grass gave way to tarmac and gravel. It also told him that he was close to the

133

network of entrances that led to the surface of The Wild. Which was where, if anywhere, he would find Daisy and the cubs.

George began to hang back deliberately. As other hamsters, voles and field mice passed, they asked if he was OK, and he had to pretend that he was just resting his paws, or looking for something that he'd dropped from one of his pouches.

'Willow, where's Willow?' he enquired, as if looking for the young shrew who was little Elsie's friend. He was gratified to hear that he was towards the back, so that he could pretend to be looking for him. Most of the rodents that passed glanced at him in wordless sympathy, and one or two of them squeezed his shoulder, but George wasn't going to give in to sympathy. That would be like admitting he'd lost everything, that he'd given up hope, whereas he was beginning to feel his hope returning. If he could just wait until everyone had passed him, he could climb to the surface and begin his search. He could see Daisy and the cubs so clearly in his mind that the image seemed real. He could almost smell them. There they were, waiting for George, and George was going to find them.

If Elsie hadn't been caught up in a rather large landslide, George's plan might never have worked. As it was, she was occupied for several minutes. Boris and Rodney helped her to scramble out, then she helped some of the smaller rodents who were trapped beneath the crumbling earth. Finally, they were ready to go on, and they trotted on quickly for several feet before Elsie remembered to check behind for George. By that time, George was nosing his way towards the surface as fast as he could.

Elsie ran backwards and forwards along the line of voles, shrews, field mice and hamsters, calling 'George! George!' Capper ran after her, asking everyone if they'd seen him. Finally Elsie stopped. 'He's not here,' she said. 'He's gone up to the surface, I know he has.'

Capper looked at her. 'What do you want to do?' he said.

'I'll go after him,' said Elsie, 'and follow my original plan. We have to trust the humans.'

Capper shook his head, but he said, 'Well, if that's the way you feel, I'm coming with you.'

'You don't have to,' Elsie began, but a chorus of voices interrupted her.

'We all want to!'

'If one of us goes, we all should!'

'We're worried about Daisy too!'

Elsie looked at Boris who had come back from the front to see what was happening.

'It's true,' he said gruffly. 'We shouldn't separate. What's left of the colony should stick together.'

Elsie looked round at them all. She felt a lump in her throat. They were so afraid of humans, but they were about to risk everything to come to the surface. She could only hope that she had been right when she said the humans could be trusted. Otherwise she would be leading them into disaster. She started to speak, then stopped. Words seemed inadequate.

'All right,' she said finally. 'Follow me.'

And she turned her nose upwards and began pushing her way through the soft earth.

The lady from the Countryside Agency had a bony, angular face, a wide curving smile and small, rather chic glasses, behind which her eyes gleamed like two copper pennies when she saw Daisy and the cubs.

'I see, I see,' she kept saying, and 'Remarkable, really remarkable!'

She walked all the way around the cardboard box, studying them from every angle.

'But can we stop the building?' Jackie wanted to know.

'Hmmm,' said the lady from the Countryside Agency. 'We can certainly *try.*'

'But you said that there were no colonies of wild hamsters that you knew of,' Jackie pointed out.

'Well, we don't know that this is a *colony* as such,' said the lady from the Countryside Agency. 'It could very well be simply a female hamster who's escaped and had her babies in The Wild.'

'Oh, I see,' said Jackie, crestfallen.

'And the other problem is,' said the lady from the Countryside Agency, 'that they're not really a *native* species, are they? From Syria originally, I think. Now if it was a great crested newt, or some house sparrows, *then* we'd be talking.'

'But can't you at least hold the building up?' said Jackie, looking more crestfallen than ever. 'Until we find out whether or not there is a colony?'

The lady from the Countryside Agency pursed her

lips so that she looked as though she was sucking a very small pea.

'Leave it with me,' she said finally. 'I'll certainly do my very best.' Her mouth expanded again into a smile. 'Meanwhile,' she said, 'these little beauties can be kept safe. We can create a special little zone for them outside.'

'Awww!' said Jake and Josh. 'Can't we keep them?'

'It's always best to return animals to their natural habitat,' said the lady from the Countryside Agency. 'But once we've created a special little reserve for them, you'll be able to visit them and to help feed them. It'll be rather like having hedgehogs in your garden!'

Jackie saw her to the front door.

'I'll phone my colleagues now,' she said, 'and try to put a halt on the building work. I can't promise anything, because hamsters aren't really *endangered*, you know, and they're definitely not native, but I'll do my very best.' She smiled bravely. 'It's just a pity we couldn't come up with anything a little more . . . *unusual*,' she said. 'But anyway, I – what's that noise?'

Both Jackie and the lady from the Countryside Agency looked round and then stared. It was Guy, holding up the traffic on the road at the far end of Bright Street. He held his lollipop sign aloft, while angry drivers tooted their horns and shouted. At first sight it looked as if no one was crossing the road; at second sight, however, Jackie noticed something moving around his feet. She looked again and gasped.

'Good grief,' said the lady from the Countryside

Agency, and 'What — ?'

But Jackie was already running towards Guy.

'Guy!' she cried. 'What's happening?'

Guy blinked several times as though he was emerging from a dream.

'Jackie,' he said, 'Frank's back — I've found Frank!'

But Jackie had crouched down and was gazing at the row of hamsters trotting quickly past. The lady from the Countryside Agency hurried towards them and she too stared in amazement. A hamster with ears just like a rabbit's ran past her foot, quickly followed by one with long, curling hair, and another one covered in fuzzy green fur like moss. Then three luminous white hamsters ran after them, glowing faintly in the dusk, and after them came the one with no fur at all, but an elephant's trunk.

'Wow!' said the lady from the Countryside Agency.

Jackie got to her feet with a little skip. 'Is that unusual enough for you?' she said to the lady from the Countryside Agency. 'Oh, well done, Guy!'

'Get a move on!' shouted one of the drivers.

'Excuse me a moment,' said Guy, and he followed the line of hamsters to the pavement of Bright Street, and once again showed them across the road. The hamsters marched with great determination across to the stretch of waste land where the builders were, and even the builders stood and stared.

'I'd never have believed it,' the overseer said. 'It's like my old mother used to say — if you can't believe something, you know it's got to be true!' And he took his hard hat off and threw it into the truck.

'But –' said the lady from the Countryside Agency. 'But you don't mean to say that they – they *live* here?'

'They do now,' said Guy, and he and Jackie watched as all the hamsters ran in and out of the grass of The Wild, nosing their way through the bracken and litter, pausing to tug at a strand of grass here and a thistle there. They all looked immediately at home. Jackie turned to Jake and Josh.

'Go and fetch the mother and her cubs,' she told them, and they ran off.

The lady from the Countryside Agency blinked very rapidly.

'I think I'd better phone my boss,' she said.

'And I'm phoning the council,' Jackie said. 'And the press!'

By the time Elsie, Boris, Capper and the rest of the colony emerged on to the surface of The Wild, a huge fuss was going on. Cars were pulling up along Bright Street and photographers climbing out. A man from the local radio station was interviewing Guy, and the boss of the building firm was locked in furious debate with the man from the council. Some of the little shrews were frightened by the commotion and immediately wanted to retreat into their burrows, but Elsie ran from one rodent to another, encouraging them to stay calm.

'Don't go!' she cried. 'We've all got to stay together or it won't work!'

'Stand together, stand together,' murmured the shrews and voles and field mice as Elsie shepherded them all into a huddle.

'No one's going to hurt you,' she said, hoping very much that it was true. 'Let them see you! This is the only way to save the colony!'

'I hope you're right,' said Boris. And he stood with Capper, Tucker and Rodney in front of the smaller rodents, looking worried and grim.

'I am right, Boris,' Elsie said earnestly. 'It's got to work – it *has* to!'

Then she squeaked aloud as the grass to one side of her parted and a huge hamster with tusks appeared, followed closely by a much smaller hamster with three ears. Boris, Tucker and Rodney reared into a threatening stance, but the strange hamsters just looked around as if dazed.

'Has anyone seen Frank?' the smaller one said.

'Frank?' whispered Elsie. 'What –?'

But she was interrupted by a commotion on the other side of the colony as Mellor appeared with his long, rabbit ears.

'Excuse me for intruding,' he said to Capper in his deep voice, and one of the voles fainted clean away. 'You wouldn't be the colony from The Wild, would you?'

'It depends who's asking,' said Capper, in a nervous, quavery voice. Then, 'Elsie?' he called, as more and more alien hamsters arrived, with green fur and glowing pelts and trunks. 'Elsie – Boris – I think we've got ourselves a situation!'

Elsie, Boris and Tucker wheeled round, but by this time they were surrounded. The strange hamsters with

trunks and tusks and long floppy ears gazed solemnly at the colony, not as if they were going to attack, but as if no one quite knew what to do next. Then suddenly, a different voice spoke.

'Where's my cage, that's what I want to know. I never said I was going to live on a dirty, muddy croft! And where's some food – I'm starving!'

'Mabel!' cried Elsie, as Mabel emerged from a tangle

of weeds. Mabel shook the bracken from her pelt. 'Disgusting!' she said. 'Are we supposed to eat dirt?' She looked around for the first time. 'Oh, hello – not you lot again,' she said.

'Mabel!' Elsie said. 'What's going on?'

'You don't want to know,' said Mabel, shaking herself again. 'What I want to know is – where's some food? And where's my nice clean bed? I'm not going to be part of this travelling freak show for much longer, I can tell you that. I don't care what Frank says –'

'Frank?' cried Elsie. 'Where is Frank?'

'Well, who cares,' Mabel began, but just then a small bush parted to Elsie's right.

'Here,' said Frank, stepping forward.

Elsie ran to him. Even as she embraced him, she couldn't help but notice how tired and worn he looked. 'Oh, Frank!' she cried, 'wherever have you been? And what's going on? Who *are* these hamsters?'

The next few moments were chaos as Frank tried to answer a hundred questions at once. All the hamsters, including the ones from the laboratory, gathered round and attempted to tell their story. Bit by bit, the whole terrible tale emerged.

'So I brought them to live here, with you,' Frank finished.

There was a silence. The hamsters from the colony looked at the hamsters from the laboratory, and then at one another. Frank felt that there was nothing else to say. They would either accept them or not. Finally, Capper stepped forward and sniffed at the hamster with curling hair and tusks.

'Well,' he said. 'It don't *look* like a hamster, but it does smell like one.'

A murmur ran through the colony. 'What did he say?'

'He said they smell like hamsters.'

'Well, if they smell like hamsters . . .'

'They must *be* hamsters!'

But the murmur was interrupted by a shout from one of the photographers.

'Oi!' he cried, 'there's more of them over here!'

The ground trembled beneath the heavy tread of human feet as several people hurried over, and there were cries of excitement.

'Look at this!'

'There's hundreds of them!'

'I've got to get a picture!'

'Stay where you are!' cried Elsie to all the trembling rodents. 'Don't move!'

And the hamsters from the laboratory huddled together with the rodents of The Wild, and all the shy, underground creatures trembled and shivered in the cold and the fading light, as all around them lights flashed and loud human voices sounded like the cawing of many birds.

'What's going on?' Frank muttered to Elsie. All his instincts were telling him to run. He felt horribly unnerved and exposed by all the attention.

'We've got to let ourselves be seen,' Elsie breathed, because she too felt very frightened. 'If they know we're here, they can't carry on with the building – Jackie said so. It's the only way to save the colony –

we've got to trust them, Frank!'

'Trust?' said Frank. 'Humans?' He felt a bitter bile in his throat. After everything he had been through and seen in the laboratory, he didn't feel as though he would ever trust another human again. Yet here they were, surrounded by humans and flashing lights. The humans didn't seem to want to hurt them – they were just being their usual clumsy, aggravating selves. It hadn't even occurred to them that creatures who were usually nocturnal wouldn't like the flashing lights and noise. But he was willing to listen to Elsie, because he simply didn't have any other ideas. He felt numb with cold and tiredness. He didn't even feel that he had the energy to run.

Then one of the humans said, 'Over here, son – bring that box,' and suddenly Frank could make out Jake, carrying a large cardboard box towards them. He set it down and lowered the cardboard flap, and all at once there was tremendous excitement.

'Daisy!' Elsie cried, and she ran towards the box, pushing her way through all the hamsters, voles and field mice who had surged towards it.

It was indeed Daisy, still surrounded by all her cubs: the big ones and the tiny babies. They looked around, bewildered, as more cameras flashed and Elsie broke through embracing first one cub then another.

'Oh, Declan! Donal! Dean! Oh, we thought you were all lost! Oh, Daisy – you're alive!'

'Course I'm alive!' said Daisy a little tartly, because she was disorientated by all the fuss. 'What is all this? Where's George?'

'George!' said Elsie, wiping her eyes as other rodents crowded forward, exclaiming over the babies. 'Yes, George – we have to find George!'

And throughout the colony, the cry went up, 'George, George!'

'We have to find George!'

'Tell him the babies are safe!'

'And Daisy!'

'Where is he – we've got to find him now!'

And forgetting the humans and the flashing lights, the rodents began to spread out, calling George's name.

And creeping from beneath a thicket of brambles, George heard. He heard all the rodents calling his name, but he didn't know what all the fuss was about.

They're trying to find me, he thought. They want me to stop looking for Daisy and go back to them.

And so he was about to turn away, ignoring them, when he heard Elsie's voice above all the others. 'George!' she shouted. 'George – we've found them! We've found Daisy and the babies!'

George felt as though his heart had stopped, then that it was turning over and over. Suddenly, he was running and tumbling towards the sound of Elsie's voice. Through thistles and bracken and over shards of glass that hurt his paws he ran and didn't stop, not even when the strong smell of human filled his nostrils. As he approached, the hamsters from the colony saw him and called his name and made a path for him all the way to the cardboard box.

'Look at this!' shouted the photographer, and 'Mum! Mum!' cried Jake and Josh, but George didn't hear. He ran into the cardboard box and straight into the arms of Daisy, hugging and nuzzling her, while Danny, Donal, Declan, Dermot, Dean and little Elsie crowded round so that they all formed one happy, tangled heap.

'I've got to get this!' the photographer said, and more cameras flashed.

'Mum!' said Jake to Jackie. 'It looks like George!'

For despite the fact that George was older now, and looked much more wild and tough than the timid pet he had once owned, Jake recognized the dark brown pelt that was so like Elsie's, and the little twist of white beneath the chin.

'Is it, Mum – is it?' Josh cried.

Jackie was smiling, though there were tears in her eyes.

'Yes, sweetie, I think it is,' she said. 'No, don't touch him!' she said as Jake's hand reached forward. 'He's got another life now.'

And she held Jake and Josh quite tightly as they crouched over the box, watching George nuzzle his new babies as Daisy nuzzled him.

Elsie made her way over to Frank.

'Oh, Frank,' she said. 'Isn't it marvellous? George and Daisy are back together again, and all these people know about the colony!'

Frank didn't answer. All these humans looming over them gave him an uncomfortable feeling, but he didn't know how to explain it. He opened his mouth to try, but at that moment they both heard Guy's voice calling, 'Frank, Frank? Has anyone seen Frank?'

Tired, cold and hungry as he was, Frank wasn't ready

to go back to his cage just yet. He darted round the side of a large stone and Elsie followed him. It was actually a little warmer there. Part of the stone stuck out over their heads and sheltered them. They watched all the noise and lights from a little distance. Water had collected on the surface of the stone and was dripping around them, but they were dry.

'Now that they know we're all here,' Elsie said, 'they'll stop the building – Jackie said so. And that means we can rebuild the New Narkiz!'

Frank looked at her. 'But all those people will know about it,' he said.

'Maybe they'll help us,' said Elsie. 'We have to trust humans some time.'

Frank didn't know if he would ever trust humans again. In the long history of the hamster race, there hadn't been that many reasons *to* trust them. Frank thought that wherever humans were, there was bound to be trouble, but he didn't want to spoil Elsie's happiness. 'Maybe,' he said.

Elsie reached out a paw and touched his face. 'You don't look well,' she said.

Frank looked at her, but he couldn't speak. His mind was full of memories of Leila. As she saw the look in his eyes Elsie's face filled with concern.

'Are you all right, Frank, dear?' she said.

Frank didn't want to explain to Elsie about Leila. He shook his head as though trying to snap out of it, and said gruffly, 'I'm all right – I'm just tired.'

But Elsie was still looking searchingly into his face. 'You look – lonely,' she said. Frank leaned back and closed his eyes. Yes, he thought. That was how he felt – lonely, and chilled through to the core. 'I'm all right,' he said again.

'Because, Frank,' Elsie said softly, 'you needn't ever feel lonely. You're surrounded by friends – and – and those who care for you very much.'

Frank opened his eyes.

'I care,' Elsie said, determined now, but stumbling over her words a little. 'More than Lucy – more than

George – I'd leave them all behind – everything – to start a new life with you – here – or anywhere.'

There, she thought, she'd said it. Frank went on looking at her and she couldn't read the expression in his eyes. Through his mind went images of this other life, different possibilities that he had never thought of before. He saw himself settling with Elsie, building a burrow, having cubs, leading the life of any hamster in The Wild. He liked Elsie, he really did. But he didn't know if she could ever fill the hollow feeling inside him. He reached out a paw and touched Elsie's face.

'I don't feel like that, Elsie,' he said.

It was hard to say it, and as he watched all the hope and longing die in her eyes, he felt more wretched than ever, but all she said was, 'No, Frank, I know you don't,' and in the silence that hung between them, they heard the water dripping from the rock above. Then Elsie said, very quietly, 'Let's join the others, shall we? You haven't seen the new cubs yet.'

She turned away, but Frank said, 'You go ahead – I'll be there in a minute.' Elsie didn't try to persuade him, she only nodded, and her eyes filled with tears, so that she couldn't look back as she hurried away.

Now Frank really was alone. What was wrong with him, he thought, that he couldn't lead a normal hamster life? Something was always pressing him on, pressing him forward, alone. And now he didn't know where it had taken him, he didn't know where he belonged, or where to go.

As if answering his thoughts, he heard Guy's voice again.

'I'm sure I saw him round here somewhere . . .'

And Jackie's voice saying, 'Well, he can't have got far – I'll help you look.'

'That's it, then,' Frank thought in a dispirited kind of way. He would climb on to the rock and allow himself to be caught. Because he knew, somehow, in the depths of his being, that he didn't want to join the New Narkiz. Not yet, anyway.

Frank climbed up the crevices in the large rock. It had rained earlier, and the surface was slippery, but he climbed doggedly until he reached the top.

From the top he could see most of The Wild. He saw all the rodents gathered round George and Daisy and the cubs: the hamsters from the laboratory and the hamsters, voles, rats, field mice, moles and shrews who were part of the colony in The Wild. He had never realized before just how many creatures had made their home there, and he blinked rapidly, taking it all in. He saw all the huge machines that had creaked to a halt quite close to him, and he saw the humans gathered round, talking earnestly amongst themselves.

'Well, if you ask me,' the lady from the Countryside Agency was saying, 'we should leave them alone now, and let them get on with it.'

'But what about my houses?' the man from the building firm was saying.

More and more humans had gathered round from all the neighbouring houses. Night was drawing in, though in fact it was only late afternoon, and above The Wild there was a heavy mass of dark cloud. Frank sniffed the air. Was that snow he could smell? Suddenly, he smelled something else, dark and wild, and he realized he wasn't alone, but he didn't turn round.

'You left me,' he said.

'Only so that you could know your own power,' said the Black Hamster of Narkiz.

Frank wasn't going to give in that easily. 'You let Leila die,' he said.

The Black Hamster was silent for a long moment, then all he said was, 'Look.'

Frank looked, and drew in his breath sharply. For there, in front of him, he could see all the rodents working together to restore the New Narkiz. All the way across The Wild they spread, building a bigger and better network of tunnels. And they were joined by more rodents, from the sewers or the pet shop, or from different houses across the town. And it wasn't only the rodents working together – the humans were helping them. They built little shelters across The Wild and filled them with food for the winter. Signs were put up and people came to visit, but they weren't allowed to interfere. He saw Guy and the children – Jake and Lucy, Thomas and Josh – showing visitors around. He saw different rodents mating and bringing up their families so that the colony thrived. Boris paired off with one of the female hamsters from the laboratory, and Frank could see little Elsie with a large, handsome hamster he recognized as Drew. Time peeled by like the layers of an onion, and he saw George and Daisy growing old together in The Wild, while Elsie came to visit them frequently. Sometimes Lucy brought her, and she always went home with her Owner. George's brood grew and multiplied and in later years he was known as the Father of The Wild. While in the centre of the Great Chamber there was a statue of a young hamster with a noble face, a hamster who had lived wild and courageous and free. With a little shock, Frank recognized himself. It was a statue of Frank.

Frank blinked away the tears in his eyes as the visions faded. He felt proud and glad, with a deep powerful gladness. He turned for the first time and looked at the Black Hamster, seeing his own gladness mirrored in the ruby eyes.

'Is it real?' he whispered, and the Black Hamster smiled.

'It's real, Frank,' he said, 'because of you.'

Frank felt a long shiver of joy along his spine. He wanted to shout and sing. It didn't matter that it wasn't the Old Narkiz, because the new one would be even better. It was there for all hamsters now.

'Will it last?' he asked. 'Will it last forever?'

The Black Hamster too was quivering with joy and pride, but all he said was, 'Forever is a long time, Frank.'

Then they beamed at one another wordlessly, and Frank felt that he never wanted that moment to end. The cold stung his eyes and he wiped away his tears with a paw. 'Well,' he said, 'what now?'

'Would you like to come with me, Frank?' said the Black Hamster.

Frank stared at him. It was as though surrounding the Black Hamster was the gateway to the Old Narkiz, in the middle of the Syrian plains, and all the hamsters that had ever lived were waiting there, for Frank.

Somewhere among them were Leila and Qita, and suddenly Frank knew that this was where he wanted to be. This was his destination and his goal.

'Yes,' he said, and he took the Black Hamster's paw.

At that moment, two things happened. Frank heard Guy's voice calling, 'There he is – there's Frank!' and he heard Guy's footsteps running towards him. At the same time the machine nearest to Frank groaned into life. The men from the building site had been ordered to clear the great machines away for now, and the shovel at the end of the digger swung towards Frank. It caught the back of his head with a sickening blow, then he was swung up, higher and higher into the freezing air.

'No! NO!' cried Guy, hurtling forward.

Frank curved into the sky in a great arc, then he was falling, falling to the stony ground. His eyes were open and he felt no pain, but darkness gathered at the edges of his vision. He saw Guy's stricken face peering into his, the mouth opening but making no sound, and far beyond Guy, the first few flakes of snow falling tenderly to the earth, like tiny stars.

13 What Happened Next

There was great and terrible mourning on The Wild.
George and Daisy clutched one another, the tears
freezing on their faces, as Guy carried Frank's body
back to his house, followed by Jackie. Elsie had seen the
whole thing. She had screamed as the digger hit Frank,
and now stood with her mouth open as though frozen
to the earth. Flakes of snow kissed her pelt and melted
there, but she felt nothing. She stood as though she'd
been turned to stone. And even Mabel, who'd been
scampering about trying to find Tania, had nothing to
say. Twice she opened her mouth, then closed it again
as the full impact of what she was seeing struck home.
She had never known death before.

Guy carried Frank away from The Wild, and all the
children clustered round. Mabel saw Tania and Lucy
and at once began to run towards them, then suddenly
she stopped, and turned back towards Elsie.

'Come on,' she said, 'you're coming with me.'

Elsie said nothing. She was shuddering with grief.
Mabel took hold of her pelt and tugged. 'You don't
belong here,' she said. 'George and Daisy have their
own life now. Come back to Lucy.'

Elsie twisted away. 'Leave me alone!' she said in a high, unnatural voice.

Mabel tugged harder. 'You'll freeze to death, child!' she said, and began dragging Elsie towards the small group of humans who were huddled around Frank.

Elsie fought. She struggled and kicked and bit. She turned her anger against Mabel, and maybe, in a way, that was safer than grief. Much to Mabel's credit, she did not let go. She was bigger than Elsie, and she used her superior weight to haul the smaller hamster through the tufts of grass, cuffing her once or twice when Elsie sank her teeth in particularly hard.

'Let me go!' Elsie shrieked, but Mabel panted, 'You're – coming – back – with – me – if – it's the – last – thing – I – do!'

She reached the group of humans just as Guy left. The photographer took a picture of him carrying Frank, just to show the kind of damage that the digging machines could do, then Guy went into number 13 Bright Street alone. Jackie stood with one arm around Tania and the other arm around Josh. All the children were trying not to cry.

Mabel wheeled Elsie round so that she struck the back of Lucy's leg with a soft thump. Lucy looked round immediately and gave a cry of joy. She had been looking everywhere for Elsie.

'Elsie! It's Elsie!'

'Mabel!' Tania cried. She too had been very afraid that she might have lost Mabel forever, when her mother told her that she had let a pair of strangers take her away. The two girls scooped their hamsters up and all the children clustered round, making a huge fuss. Lucy was so pleased to see Elsie that she kept kissing her and pressing her to her face. Elsie stopped struggling and allowed herself to sink into Lucy's palms. She closed her eyes and heard Jackie's voice saying, 'She looks frozen to death, poor thing! Mabel too. You'd better take them both inside and get them nice and warm.'

'And give them lots to eat,' said Mabel, but Elsie wasn't listening. She just wanted to shut it all out and sink into oblivion. As Lucy carried her away, the last thing she heard was the voice of the lady from the

Countryside Agency talking to the man from the local radio.

'Of course it takes a tragedy like this,' she was saying as he recorded her, 'to make people sit up and realize the damage that's being done . . .'

But that was the last thing she heard, because Lucy carried her inside, to light and warmth, and tucked her very gently into her cage . . .

. . . And Elsie slipped into a deep, dark sleep. She had never hibernated before, because she lived in a warm room, but she now sank into a state that was deeper than sleep, punctuated by very short, shifting dreams, and when she finally woke after several days, the air and atmosphere around her felt quite different. It wasn't spring yet, but it was one of those soft, warm patches that sometimes happen in the middle of even the coldest winter. From her cage, as she nosed her way out of her bedroom, she could sense new life stirring outdoors. And her first thoughts weren't of Frank or George, but food. She was starving! She climbed out of bed and ate enormously.

Only when she had finished a huge meal, full of sunflower seeds and peanuts and broccoli that Lucy brought to her because she was so pleased to see Elsie up and about again, did Elsie begin to feel the sense of loss and pain. She stopped eating, and stared mournfully out of the window. Grieving for Frank wouldn't bring him back, she knew, and she also knew, being a very sensible hamster, that even if she *could* bring him back, he wouldn't be coming back to her. Still, what she felt was a hollowness, as though something vital and central in her life had gone forever.

And she couldn't help but wonder how George was taking it.

So one night, when she felt a bit stronger, she opened the door of her cage.

'I won't be long, Lucy,' she said, looking at the sleeping child, who worried so much about her when she was gone. She hoped, in fact, to be back before Lucy woke up, because Elsie, more than all the hamsters, knew what it was really like to miss someone.

Down the stairs she crept. She had learned a lot about leaving her home now. She knew how to make her way through the little grid in the front room to the Spaces Between, and to get from there to the little grid that led on to the pavement. She knew to sniff cautiously for the scent of cats before squeezing herself through, and to distinguish between all the different scents of the outside world once she was on the pavement. She could tell, for instance, though the air always smelled of petrol, whether or not a car was approaching, and only when she was quite sure it was safe did she trot quickly across the gravel and tarmac and cobbles of the road.

All her senses were alert as she reached The Wild. She could smell that foxes had been prowling, but were not close now, and that a big bird, maybe an owl, had passed overhead recently. Then she pushed her way through the bracken and came across something she had not smelled before. It was a wooden box, and the wood smelled new. And the box itself was full of food

– seed and bacon rind and leaves of various kinds. It was one of the shelters that the children had made and filled with food to help the hamsters and other small creatures through the winter.

Elsie paused to tuck a little more food into her pouches. Then she sniffed the air again. She could smell that she was near one of the many openings that led to the network of tunnels beneath The Wild. She travelled quickly now, entering the warm burrow and nosing her way through until she reached a mass of rubble. She pushed and kicked and scrabbled until she found her way into an adjacent burrow, and followed that until the same thing happened.

Elsie was puzzled. She had thought that all the rebuilding would have been done by now, and the network of tunnels that led to the Great Chamber restored, but she followed one tunnel after another but each ended in rubble. Finally she came across a family of sleeping voles. She shook one of them gently by the pelt.

'Where's the Great Chamber?' she asked. 'Where's George?'

But the vole only shook his head sleepily and shrugged his shoulders.

'Over there somewhere,' he mumbled, and curled up again into sleep.

Elsie pushed on through rubble and finally came to a space that opened out into what must have been the ruins of the Great Chamber. She crawled through the rubble, staring. No work had been done at all. The pillars had collapsed, the stone on which Frank had stood to make his first speech to the new colony had disappeared, and everywhere was deathly quiet. Elsie couldn't understand it. She pushed on in the direction that she remembered George's burrow had been.

There at last she heard a scrabbling noise and some hushed voices. A twitching nose appeared through the rubble, and soon a young female hamster emerged, followed by a small shrew. They stopped and stared at Elsie, then the young hamster said slowly, 'Why, it's Aunty Elsie!' and ran forward to hug her.

'Little Elsie?' Elsie cried, but her niece was little no more. She was, if anything, slightly bigger than her aunt. She looked as pretty as ever, but scruffy and ungroomed.

'I'm so glad I've found you – I was beginning to think this place was deserted,' Elsie said. 'Where's your father – where's George?'

Little Elsie sighed. 'Mum and Dad don't hardly come out of their burrow these days,' she said. 'No one does – they all keep saying it's time to hibernate.'

'But – there's so much work to be done,' Elsie said, staring round at the ruined hall.

'I know – but no one wants to do it. We don't meet up no more, and Dad just keeps saying, "There'll be time one day." It's like he doesn't care.' Little Elsie sighed and her eyes were sad. Then she brightened. 'He'll be pleased to see you though,' she said. 'Shall I take you to him?'

'I think you'd better,' Elsie said. Little Elsie spoke to the shrew, who ran off to fetch some food, then she led her aunt through the remains of the Great Chamber.

'That's Willow – he's my friend,' she said over her shoulder. 'He's the only one who'll play with me – it's really boring. I'm so glad you've come! Mum and Dad'll have to wake up now.'

'How are the babies?' Elsie asked, picking her way carefully through the fallen earth and stones.

'Babies are fine,' little Elsie said, as if she didn't really care one way or another. 'That's all Mum and Dad ever think about now. It's all, "Oh, we can't leave the babies," and "We've got to keep the babies warm!" Most of the time they don't even get up.'

Elsie shook her head. She couldn't believe that George was letting things slide like this, after everything the colony had been through. He must be really unhappy, she thought, and felt a pang of sadness herself. But her heart lifted as she approached the burrow, with its familiar scents of George and Daisy, mingled with the new scents of baby hamsters. As she entered the burrow she could see that they were all curled up together in a tangled heap, sleeping. One of the baby hamsters was trying to crawl over the others towards his mother for milk.

'Mum, Dad!' little Elsie called out as they entered. 'Surprise!'

George opened one eye blearily. 'Not now,' he mumbled, then he stopped and opened the other eye. 'Why – it's Elsie!'

'It certainly is!' said Elsie bracingly, and she stepped right over two of the smallest cubs and hugged George as hard as she could.

'Elsie – Elsie!' said George in amazement. 'Daisy –

wake up,' he said, 'it's Elsie!'

For the next few minutes, Elsie hugged George and Daisy and all the little cubs in turn, admiring her new nieces (there were five of them) and little nephew (the one who had been trying to crawl over the others towards his mum).

'Oh, they're beautiful, George – they're gorgeous!' Elsie exclaimed, kissing the baby cubs over and over as they squirmed and kicked and tried to get away. Daisy beamed and George laughed modestly. 'Heh heh heh,' he said.

'What are their names?' Elsie wanted to know, and George looked sheepish.

'Er – well,' he said. 'We – er – haven't picked any yet.'

Elsie stared at him in astonishment. '*Haven't picked any?*' she repeated in disbelief. She was about to ask, 'Well, what have you been doing then?' but at that moment Willow returned with the food.

'Sit down with us and have something to eat,' Daisy said, remembering her manners and clearing a space for their guest.

Elsie, Daisy and George sat and ate and talked while little Elsie kept an eye on the squirming, fighting cubs. It seemed that, since that terrible day when Frank had gone, everyone in the colony had lost heart. They had stood around in the snow, not knowing what to do, and finally, in danger of freezing, had crept away silently and separately, into different burrows. They knew that the building had stopped, so the colony was safe, and that the humans were leaving them food in little boxes, without which the laboratory hamsters might not have survived at all. But it was as if, now the danger was over, no one had the energy to start again. And it was winter, the time when every wild animal withdraws into itself, conserving energy until the sun returns.

'But, George,' Elsie said, 'there's so much to do!'

George looked sheepish. 'I know,' he said, and mumbled something about not knowing where to start.

'Well, you have to start somewhere,' Elsie said. 'And you have to start now.'

George and Daisy looked at one another and away. Daisy began to concentrate on grooming the little boy cub.

'George —' Elsie said helplessly. Then she said, 'Come with me — come on.'

George looked questioningly at Daisy, but she didn't look up, and Elsie was tugging him by the pelt. He followed her along the half-collapsed burrow to the ruins of the Great Chamber.

'This is where you start,' said Elsie.

George sat down heavily. 'I can't,' he said.

'What do you mean — you can't?'

George shook his head and sighed as Elsie glared at him.

'Look, George,' she said. 'Just look at all this. You built it all and it was great — it was marvellous. And now you've got to do it again. Because this is the heart of the colony. Without a Great Chamber you can't have meetings or celebrations — or — anything. Without this there *is* no colony. So this is where you start. I know it's a lot of work, but at least this time you know it'll be safe.'

George was still sighing and shaking his head.

'You'll need help, of course,' Elsie went on. 'But you've got Boris and Tucker and Rodney; you all need to work together to make it just as good as it was – or better!'

George still said nothing. Elsie went right up to him and clasped her paws around his cheeks. 'George,' she said quietly. 'What is it?'

'I can't!' he burst out miserably and for a moment Elsie thought he was going to dissolve into tears, but all he said was, 'Leave me alone,' and he tried to turn away, but Elsie gripped him hard.

'Listen to me, George,' she said even more quietly. 'You can – because you've got to. You think I don't know –?' she said, her voice rising a little shakily because she too felt tears threatening. 'You think I don't miss him?' She couldn't bring herself to say Frank's name, but she steadied herself and went on. 'I miss him more than you know. But this – this is no way to remember him. You can't just sit around and *mope*! What would Frank say if he could see all this now – what would he do?' And when George still said nothing, she said, 'Are you going to tell me that he died for nothing?'

'Don't say that,' George said, dashing a tear from his eye.

'Well – what then?' Elsie said, and now she was crying too. 'Tell me, George, what is it – what's the matter?'

George sighed even more heavily than before and there was a long silence. Then he said, 'I – I don't know what it is, Elsie. I'm sorry, I really am, but – I'm not a leader, I suppose.'

Elsie stared at him. 'What?' she said.

'I'm not a leader – I can't lead the colony. I – I'm not Frank.'

Elsie thought that was stating the obvious, but she waited.

'I know I got everything going before, all the building and stuff,' George said, 'but somehow – I think I was really doing it all for Frank – all the time – I thought Frank'd come and he'd think it was marvellous and want to stay here and – and, well – that's why I was so disappointed when he did come and he didn't seem to like it or want to stay.'

It was Elsie's turn to shake her head. 'Poor George,' she said softly.

'I told myself that Frank would be the leader and he could take the decisions – I'm not like that, Elsie – I'm no hero – I'm just a quiet chap who wants to look after his family and lead a quiet life. Frank is – *was* – the natural choice to lead us all. But now he's gone.' And George sniffed wetly and a tear plopped to the ground.

Elsie was silent for a moment, then she said, 'Did you never think, George, that it might not be about one hamster leading others? I mean – wasn't that what Frank said – that you all had to work together and everyone take responsibility for everything? Maybe that's why he didn't stay – because he knew you'd all want him to be the leader.'

George looked up at her, but he didn't say anything.

'I mean – isn't that what this place is all about?' she went on. 'You don't live with humans now, you live together, and you have to join forces. It's no good thinking like – like servants and slaves; you're all equal here and you have to think like a free hamster. If you have leaders then no one'll be free.'

George still said nothing, but he was listening.

'You have to remember what Frank said,' Elsie urged. 'You have to build this place again – as he would have wanted it – and never, never forget him, George.' She stroked his face and forehead and looked deeply into his eyes, and from nowhere the word she wanted came to her. 'Courage,' she said.

Now George looked back at Elsie and his own eyes began to shine.

'We could build something,' he said, 'to remember him by!'

'A memorial stone.'

'Or a statue!'

'And you could put what he said about the colony beneath it, for everyone to see!'

'We could put it in the centre of the Great Chamber,' George said, getting excited now, 'and that's where we'll all meet –' He broke away from Elsie and began to look at the ruins of the Great Chamber. 'It shouldn't take too long to clear the rubble,' he said.

'That's it, George! That's it!' cried Elsie and her eyes filled with tears again, but this time they were tears of joy. 'Once you get started, it won't take any time at all!'

George turned to face Elsie, and already he looked a

different hamster.

'Let's go and tell Daisy,' he said. 'And – and we'll name those cubs! I know what I want to call the little lad –'

Elsie knew too. 'Frank,' she whispered and George nodded. He took her paw in his. 'Let's get going,' he said. 'There's work to be done!'

Meanwhile, the humans had been busy too. With the help of the police and Mrs Wheeler, who was really very sorry that she had given Mabel away, the lady from the Countryside Agency had tracked down Marcia Taylor and Vernon Maid and they had both been arrested for practising unnatural activities without a licence. The police had found lots of files on their computer dedicated to tracking down hamsters in different areas. Everyone who had ever clicked on their website, which offered a chat room and a lot of free information about hamsters, had been asked to give their address, and name a friend who also owned a hamster. In this way the scheming pair had gained a lot of detail about people who owned hamsters. After they were arrested, the police gave a talk in the local community centre about the dangers of chatting on the web and about never, ever giving an address.

The lady from the Countryside Agency managed to get some money from the Department of the Environment to turn The Wild into a protected area, or Pocket Park, because, she insisted, it was a site of special conservational interest. This meant that it couldn't be built on, and that members of the public could come and visit it and buy bags of food to leave for the small creatures in special shelters. And she even asked Guy if he would take charge of the site and distribute information.

'We can pay a small wage,' she said. 'Not very much, but it would be good to have someone who actually *lives* here to act as a sort of *custodian*.'

Poor Guy was still shattered by the loss of Frank, and he had caught a terrible cold, so he didn't sound very enthusiastic.

'I'll think about it,' he said, and went back to lying on his settee in front of the television with a big box of hankies by his side. He didn't even have the heart to pick up his guitar. And every time he thought of Frank, or looked at the empty cage that he hadn't been able to bring himself to throw away, he had to blow his nose again.

Eventually Jackie called round with a pan full of chicken soup.

'For the invalid,' she said, and sat down on the edge of the settee where he lay. 'Do you think you'll get another hamster?' she said, glancing at the empty cage.

Guy shook his head vigorously. 'Definitely not,' he said thickly, through a hanky. 'I've had them before, you know – Frank was the only one that lasted, and now he's gone. And, well, he was special. I'll never replace him.'

Jackie took hold of his hand. There was a different look in her eyes – a kind of warmth. 'I think it's really nice that you cared about Frank so much,' she said.

'He was my best friend,' Guy said, and there was a

catch in his voice. 'Sometimes I think he was my only friend.'

'Oh, now, that's not true,' Jackie said. 'You've got your friends in the band, and – and, well – there's me.'

She blushed as she said it and looked down at his hand that lay between both of hers.

Guy stared at her. 'Do you mean it?' he asked.

'Of course I do!' said Jackie. 'You mean a lot to me – and to the kids, of course.'

It was Guy's turn to blush. 'Thanks,' he said.

'And what I was coming to tell you,' she said, still looking at his hands rather than his face, 'is that they're looking for a new band at The Angel, and the landlord, Derek, asked me if I knew anyone, and I told him about you – and he wants to know if you can play there Friday night!'

Guy sat up on the settee, looking as if he couldn't quite believe it. 'Are you sure?' he asked.

'Definitely.' Jackie said. 'So you'd better get some of that chicken soup down you, and start phoning your friends!'

'That's amazing!' Guy said. 'That's – well – thanks!'

'Don't mention it,' Jackie said, smiling as she got up. 'In fact – I thought we could go over there together later on to see Derek and have a drink.'

Guy stared at her. 'What, you and me – together?' he said.

'Well – yeah – if you want to, that is.'

'If I *want* to?' Guy said in amazement. 'Well, of course I want to – I just didn't think you'd want to,' he added.

'Oh, well,' said Jackie, opening the door. 'I just reckon that any bloke who cares that much about his hamster can't be all bad,' and she left, still smiling. Guy stared after her. It all seemed a bit like a dream. First the offer to look after The Wild, then maybe a regular gig for his band at the pub, and now this – him and Jackie, going out together!

For the first time in days Guy picked up his guitar. He plucked the strings absent-mindedly. Automatically he thought of Frank, for whom he had composed so many songs, and the plucking became a gentle strum. And soon, words came to him, and a tune very similar to one his mother had taught him long ago, and he began to sing:

> *Oh, Frankie boy,* he sang,
> *The pipes, the pipes are calling.*

It didn't sound quite right, so he revved up the tune a little, into a rock and roll beat.

> *But come you back*
> *When summer's in the meadow*
> *Or when the val-ley's*
> *Hushed and white with snow . . .*

Then he added an exciting riff, that was sweet and mournful all at once.

> *And I'll be there*
> *In sunshine or in sha-adow*

Oh, Frankie boy, oh, Frankie boy
We love you so . . .

And when, later that night, he played it for his friends in the band, they all joined in, improvising guitar and drum solos around the basic tune. And the audience at The Angel loved it, and so did audiences at several other pubs in the town. Even the old people in the care homes loved it and joined in, and soon it seemed that the whole town was singing 'Frank's Song', and the band had their first popular hit.

So that was the story of the hamsters of Bright Street. It went on, as all good stories do, even after the final page. When Mr Marusiak came back, for example, he asked Mrs Timms to marry him and she said yes, and they lived together very happily in number 1 Bright Street, thereby solving the problem of difficult tenants and of stray cats, since all the cats lived with them, and were not allowed to prowl across The Wild. This meant that the house next door to Jackie's, number 7, was now empty, but in the fullness of time Guy moved into it, and they began turning the two separate houses into one. And number 13 Bright Street was turned into a kind of visitors' centre, containing information on all the small creatures who lived in The Wild and how to help them thrive. Many people visited, not just from the local area, but all over England. And gradually, as the fame of the first hamster colony spread, there were visitors from all the different countries in the world.

Meanwhile George and Daisy had restored the New Narkiz with the help of Boris and Capper and the others in The Wild. Because they had all worked on it, they all felt they belonged there, even the laboratory hamsters, and none of them ruled over the others. They settled with mates and had families, and their children, and their children's children grew and multiplied.

Elsie visited often, and was a great favourite with her many nieces and nephews, because she always brought special treats from the human world and kept them in touch with what was happening. She was there when the statue to Frank was unveiled, and when little Elsie made her own burrow with Drew, and they had their first litter of cubs. But she was always happy to return to Lucy, and Lucy was always very happy to see her when she came home.

Mabel grew quite old and fat, and pampered as ever, especially by Mrs Wheeler, who had been horrified when she had learned what Marcia Taylor and Vernon Maid were really up to. It took Tania a long time to forgive her, and she tried hard to make up for what she'd done by cooking Mabel special meals three times a day, and installing a little mirror in her bedroom, so that Mabel could admire herself without moving. From time to time Elsie, remembering how Mabel had saved her on the terrible night of Frank's death, visited her and told her all the news of The Wild. Mabel was quite content with this, and had no desire to visit herself, or to leave her luxurious cage ever again. She looked forward to

Elsie's visits, though she would never have admitted it. They often sat and talked together about the old times, and about Frank. And Mabel talked about Frank as though he had been her best friend, instead of a dangerously mad rodent, and as though she had given him lots of useful advice. Elsie didn't bother to correct her, and if she felt a pang whenever Frank's name was mentioned, she kept that to herself, deciding, like the very sensible hamster she was, that while she couldn't have *everything* she wanted, she in fact had a life she liked, and a lot of people (and hamsters) that she loved. So that really, she was a very lucky hamster indeed.

And now it only remains for me to tell you about one further incident, which took place in another part of the same town. There in a small house that overlooked a field, lived a hamster called Gary. He had been bought from Mr Wiggs's Pet Shop just a few days before by a little boy called Robbie, but he didn't really feel settled. He spent his nights moving his bed around and swinging on the bars of his cage, or gnawing at them restlessly. He didn't know what it was that wouldn't let him settle, only that his cage seemed too small for him somehow, and that he had the urge to break free.

Then one night, after everyone in the family had gone to sleep, he heard a voice.

'Gary,' it said.

Gary reared, sniffing the air. He could see nothing, but he heard the voice again. 'Gary.'

There was something strange, and yet familiar, about
the voice – something old and beckoning and sweet.
He wasn't afraid of it at all, yet he felt his spine tingle
when it spoke to him.

'Gary.'

'Who are you?' he managed to ask.

'Look around you, Gary,' said the voice. Gary
looked, and there on the table just outside his cage, was
another hamster. He was a little larger than Gary and
such a bright, deep golden colour that he actually
glowed.

'Who are you?' Gary asked again, though something

told him that he knew. 'Are you – are you the Golden Hamster of Narkiz?'

He didn't know where the knowledge had come from, but he knew it was true. The other hamster smiled, a bright, warm smile.

'If you like,' he said, 'but you can call me Frank.'

Very good books about Very bad children

Little Darlings

SAM LLEWELLYN

A very good book about very bad children

Also available on Puffin Audio

SAM LLEWELLYN

Bad, Bad Darlings

Small But Deadly

Another Very good book about very bad children

Illustrations © David Roberts

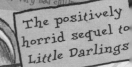

Dear Intelligent Reader

You are cordially invited to a marvellous comic extravaganza in which Solomon Snow sets out to find his true parents.

Thrill at his quest to track down his silver spoon.

Gasp as our hero triumphs over rogues and vagabonds... even though his boots pinch and it's always raining.

Marvel as he finds his destiny — but will it really mean wearing purple velvet pantaloons?

Find out in
The Silver Spoon of Solomon Snow

Nerve-tingling, fast-paced adventure with bite!

Count Muesli is the hottest veggie vampire in town. Banished by the evil Count Fibula, Count Muesli must leave Eyetooth. But when his human friends are captured by Fibula, he braves all the dangers and returns to Eyetooth to save them.

Dracula is *so* last century!